Sphinxlike Bonds

Marina Motamed

Title: Sphinxlike Bonds
Author: Marina Motamed
Illustrator: Krisna Satria Febrianto

ISBN 978-1-915557-04-9
eISBN 978-1-915557-05-6

Firouz Media Limited
www.firouzmedia.com
IG: @firouzmedia

Chapter One

Grace walked on the sidewalk, her mind drifting off to other things. She was a woman who took control of things; some sort of independence oozing off her. She had her silky black hair in an alternative, layer style, and a violin case in her hand. Her headphones blasted music in her ears as she nodded in sync with the beat.

She was in her twenties, with her whole life ahead of her. One would say she had all the time in the world with the way she carried herself. Her striped black and white socks were a little bit visible through her loose black trousers and black shoes to match. She walked even slower as soon as she saw the bus stop. Ordinarily, a person would quicken the pace to get there faster, but Grace was not one of such persons. Even though she was barely twenty steps away from where the bus stop was, she wasn't perturbed. Her life was usually that way, spent in no hurry, her own style of taking things one at a time with the moment. She faced life with that same perspective, seeing no need to rush anything. She got to the bus stop and stood there for a few minutes, staring at the timetable of when the buses would arrive. She checked and found out that she had little time to spare. A quaint grocery shop was right behind the bus stop, so she decided to spend her time there.

She walked into the grocery shop with an air of confidence that couldn't be faked. She exuded it. The way she walked, the way she carried herself, everything screamed of a woman who was at home in her own body. She didn't bother with others, for all she cared, she was all that mattered.

She found a newspaper on display and grabbed one. The headlines were ranting about the state of the economy but she ignored it. She folded it once to be able to hold it well, went to the fridge to grab a bottle of vegetable detox juice, and held it with her fingers to be able to handle the violin case without its contents spilling on the floor. It was more of a herculean task than she thought, but she managed to do it anyway. She got to the counter and paid the cashier, and she walked out of the place, hoping the bus would have arrived by the time she was outside.

As it turned out, the bus had pulled up by the sidewalk, and Grace was among the first few people to enter. It was Bus 102. She heaved a sigh of relief as she got on the bus, she didn't fancy waiting for too long and was glad she didn't have to. It would have grated on her nerves to no end.

Life was good to her, not overly stressful at least. She could live at her pace, do things when she wanted to, and maybe that kind of life wouldn't have appealed to most, but it was pure bliss to Grace. In the bus, as it started to move, she watched the scenery fly past, turning into a moving stream of colors. She leaned back, closed her eyes, and allowed the music from her headphones to immerse her into another world unknown.

***

A beautiful sound was emanating from a studio as Grace and five other musicians played to their heart's content. The sound of a saxophone, the striking of a key on the piano, the soft but soulful sound coming from the guitar, the drum on a steady rhythm like a beating heart, and the sound of a cello running through riffs. The studio was a mess, bags, mobile phones, coats and various bottles of soft drinks laid all over the floor with no one to take them. It was a studio, but with the trash, it was unlike one.

Tom, a sometimes eccentric guy, played a wrong note on the piano that more or less put a halt to the rehearsal. A handsome face to go with his black-rimmed glasses, he was a perfect picture of a gentleman.

He gave a shy smile and made his fingers into a gun and made a show of putting a bullet through his skull. He laughed while doing so.

"Need a break." He managed to say as an excuse to assuage the guilt, knowing that the rehearsal had come to an end for that day. Not like anybody was complaining though. They'd been at it for a while.

Grace took a quick look at the state of the surroundings and put her violin in its case, trying to pick things up as she went. It wasn't hard for her. The place screamed with an urgency to be clean, to be rid of the dirt that had been strewn all over it, and Grace answered that call.

"Yes, coffee!" Grace said to herself as she made her way to the kitchen, straight to the coffee machine.

She poured a cup of coffee and turned off the coffee machine. Tom came into the kitchen holding an empty cup. She sighed.

"You've got to wait." She said to Tom as soon as he entered the kitchen

She took the filter out, threw out the coffee grinds, washed the filter, and dried it with a kitchen roll. It wasn't hard to do, she did it like it was second nature to her. That was how it was with habits. She added coffee to it. Tom filled the coffee machine with water while she worked.

"Can't wait to take you out for dinner... tonight?" He spoke smiling, trying to ask her out once again. It was a running joke that hell would freeze over before she accepted him but she wasn't perturbed. Not in the least.

"This again... Don't start." She chided, concentrating on her work with disinterest in Tom.

Her words didn't seem to make his smile budge from his face. It was as though Grace's words only made him beam brighter.

"Come on, Grace, give me a better reason for turning me down?" Tom pressed, his voice soft so as not to turn off Grace.

But she wasn't in the mood for his flirting, she did want to hear anyone tell her a word about love, or how they felt about her. And one such person was Tom. Maybe another time, if she was up to it, but at that moment, he was nothing but a nuisance.

"I am not ready for this." She said firmly, brokering no room for discussion. She wasn't always like this, cold and uncaring. On some days, she listened to him and tried to humor him, but today was different, something was out of place, and she wasn't feeling up to it, to his advances and she didn't want to bother lying about it.

She grabbed her cup immediately, and walked out, leaving Tom in the kitchen, dejected and left to figure himself out. She hated leading people on, especially Tom, though he had good intentions, she just wasn't ready for such and she'd said as much on various occasions. But, he was just too stubborn to listen, and would always come back, asking her the same, "Can I take you out tonight?"

Grace was having so much fun with the other members of the band. Sara, the woman who played the cello, was even more excited. Her voice came out in a high-pitched fervor. It was a good rehearsal, even better than what Grace expected. The other members of the band had the same thought too.

"Yes! Done. Let's go out for a pint. What do you say?" Sara asked the group at large and their response was in the affirmative.

"Yes!" They said in unison as Sara clapped her hands with glee. She ushered them out of the studio dramatically as Grace laughed.

***

Grace placed her violin between her legs as she held back a sigh of exhaustion. She could feel sweat forming on her thighs so she placed her hands on them, making it as though to wipe the sweat droplets away. She felt as if the energy in her was sapped by something, her breaths were now heavy, and she felt like laying down. The others continued with their drinking, oblivious to Grace's dilemma.

"I'm going home." Grace could no longer stand it and the jovial air in the atmosphere dampened a bit. Sara looked at her with concerned, searching eyes.

"Oh, please.." Sara tried to dissuade her, but Grace wasn't one to be swayed and she knew that much.

"I'm sorry, I really have things to do. Another time, okay, guys?" Grace said in an apology to Sara. She placed her hand over Sarah, enveloping her in a hug, promising to come back. Sara returned her hug.

"Promise?" Sara asked once more and Grace nodded in the affirmative which was apparently good enough for Sara.

She waved to Sara and the others with a smile on her face as she started packing her stuff to go home. She moved swiftly and was out the door in minutes.

***

Grace got to her house in the evening. She shut the door behind her as she entered, making sure to lock up. She put her violin case aside, bending down to pick a mail that was on the floor. While walking down the corridor, she opened the envelope.

Her flat was minimalistic, with white painted walls, a large, conceptual black and white painting, and long white curtains. She wasn't the type of person to bother about frivolities, she hated them in fact. She was practical to a fault. There were no pictures hanging on the walls in the flat; not a single one. There was a big pot of tulips on the kitchen counter and white orchids on the coffee table. Just the way she liked it.

She went to the kitchen, pouring herself a glass of wine. She left the letters on the counter, grabbed the remote control next to the tulips, and turned on the TV. She made sure she was comfortable as she sat on the sofa and started watching a foreign movie *Woman in the Dunes* part way through.

While she was focused on the movie, her phone rang loud enough to disrupt her concentration. She hesitated for a few seconds before and finally decided to answer it after deliberating within herself, and when it seemed the call wouldn't stop coming.

She paused the movie as she circled the air with the glass of wine, watching as the gold-yellow liquid swirled in the glass, wondering what was going on for her to receive a call.

"It's been okay, you?" She responded to the other person on the line, not betraying who it was. There was an air of mystery around her.

"It's your birthday, right?" She asked, wincing a little. The person on the other end of the call seemed to be boiling with rage, even though the words coming from the phone weren't heard. Grace's reaction was clear.

"I can't believe, after so many years, you still don't get that I am not good at remembering dates." She said in a bid to pacify the person on the line but she had to hold her phone away from her ears as screams came hurling through it. The person on the other end didn't seem pleased. Grace waited till the person was calm before she continued.

"Okay, okay.. I'll be there." She placed the phone back to her ear, drinking the last drop of wine in her glass. She stood up a whole later, and made her way to the bedroom, with her phone pressed to her ear. She turned off the tv as an afterthought.

"Barbecue... sure! Next Saturday... Sounds great." She ended the call and gave a sigh of relief. Then she plopped on the bed and covered her face with a pillow.

Chapter Two

Grace and Tom are in a cozy, dimly lit restaurant. They are having cocktails. There was an air of tranquility. It was a moonlit night.

"Seems like this isn't the dinner I expected." Tom broke the silence, a mock-serious expression on his face.

"Of course not. I can't believe we are still talking about this." Grace chided, unable to continue fanning the flames of his antics. Tom was handsome, sure. But he came on too strong and it was sometimes irksome to her.

"Tom, can you be serious now? We want you to come to do a piano quartet." Grace continued, stopping him from speaking. She knew that he wanted to continue the conversation in a light she didn't like.

"With your string trio?" Tom asked, musing. A hand was placed on his chin in a gesture of being lost in thought.

"We would like you to play a Schumann piece," Grace said, matter-of-factly. Tom was good at what he did and she wasn't going to deny that for any reason.

"I always wanted to do something with you guys…" Tom

trailed off, giving it some thought. It'd help him while away the time at the very least. And maybe he'd find a minute or two with Grace.

"Good. Let's order, then I'll talk you through it. I'm so hungry." Grace said, after realizing that Tom was going to do it after all.

She called the waiter over and placed her order.

***

Grace was driving through a tunnel in the afternoon, jazz music coming from the speakers of her car as she nodded her head in tune with the rhythm, pausing at a particular part. It was a song by *Melody Gardot,*

My soul is weary
Beaten down from all of my misery, yeah
Oh Lord, who will comfort me?

Grace rewinds that part, singing along as she drove. She was giddy. She kept singing as she went, feeling the moment even more. The ride was a truly enjoyable one.

She got to her destination, a house. She drove her car into the car space right beside the house, shutting off the engine as she made her way out of the car.

She got into the house, and walked down the hallway to see different people all over the place. It was a whole crowd. She tried to navigate her way around the mass of people, from the kitchen to the living room. There were people everywhere. Drinking, laughing, and whatnots. It was clear she was looking for someone but she hadn't found that person yet.

She made her way out of the house and to the garden. There she sees a woman; Jade. She was wearing grey men's shorts and a white shirt, with a small orange scarf around her neck. She was preparing the barbecue. A smile morphed onto her face when she saw Grace.

"Hey, long time no see." She called out to Grace who smiled right back before she answered.

"Hey."

Jade pulled Grace into a hug, and Grace allowed herself to be pulled along. A blonde girl stood by the side watching them and she caught Grace's eye. Grace noticed her staring and she had to ask Jade who the girl was.

"Who's she?" She asked.

"She's the girl I'm dating," Jade said with a faded smile playing on her face. She turned and gave the girl a call.

Hailey was fixing her drink. She wore a light blue shirt and soft black roll-up trousers, along with comfortable light blue boat shoes. She turned, with a smile, at the sound of Jade's voice and left her glass on the table. Hailey walked gracefully towards them.

"Grace, my lovely friend, and my favorite violinist." Jade gestured to Grace as Grace ducked her head shyly.

Grace watched Jade as she did the introductions between the two. They shook hands warmly, even though they'd not met each other prior to that day.

"Nice to meet you, finally. I was starting to think Jade

had an imaginary friend." Hailey teased Jade, making all laugh.

"Don't listen to her too much, she can be like that sometimes. Hailey, my girlfriend." Jade gestured to Hailey and they shared a look that seemed a little too intimate.

"Nice to meet you too. And yes, I do exist. When I'm not in my cave, that is.." Grace said, keeping a smile on her face.

Jade tapped Grace on the shoulder and she involuntarily flinched. She hated that, even though she wasn't vocal about it, it was clear from her facial features.

"I'm happy you could make it today," Jade said with as much sincerity as she could muster. Jade noticed even though she didn't say anything about it. She put on her gloves and added more coal to the barbecue.

"Hey, thanks for inviting me," Grace said to Jade, already feeling guilty from the way she acted a few moments before Hailey came to her rescue.

She stared at Grace and decided to bail her out, "Why don't you come with me? I'll show you the minibar. Actually, I was in the middle of fixing myself a drink."

Grace almost heaved a sigh of relief, jumping at the opportunity.

"Sure." She replied, and Hailey turned to Jade, sharing another intimate look as she touched her softly.

"Would you want me to bring you a drink?" she asked

Jade, but she declined. Hailey was then pulled into a kiss, an overly intimate one, with their eyes closed, oblivious of who stared, or who stood close.

"I'm alright for now, I'll grab a beer later on," Jade said to Hailey, who nodded with a warm smile as she began to lead Grace to the place where they'd have their drinks.

"Thanks." Grace's voice came out in a small tone as she followed Hailey to the gazebo, at a loss for what to say.

The good thing was that Hailey knew her way around. She fixed the drink for the both of them and casually struck up a conversation while she added an ice cube to her drink.

"You know, whenever Jade talks about you, she gets this smile on her face," Hailey said, with an ever-green smile. Grace didn't know what to make of the conversation so she went ahead with it.

"I don't know what to say." She smiled as she added a tonic to her drink. She raised her glass and clinked it against Hailey's. "I'm just glad I get to meet you, and I'm really happy for you guys," Grace added, and Hailey stared at her for a few seconds, her eyes narrowed. She tried to change the subject almost immediately and needed anything to change the subject. She looked around and found Grace's hair. It was quite a messy, short and layered haircut. As though she didn't give much thought to her hairstyle. That gave her a kind of individuality that was hard to replicate. It was cool actually.

"Thanks. By the way, I like your hair." Hailey said with sincerity and Grace's eyes lit up.

"It's all my hair stylist's doing. I don't show him a picture of a model or anything like that, I just tell him what I feel I need. Like last time, I said I want femininity, gentleness, and power. And the result just… felt right. Yesterday I told him I need a change…" Grace stopped momentarily, realizing that she'd spoken more than she originally intended. She took a sip of her drink, unable to meet Hailey's eyes after realizing her folly.

"Interesting! A change. In what way?" Hailey asked, genuinely curious. Grace didn't like where the conversation was going and felt strangely self-conscious. She didn't understand it herself.

"Oh, it's a long story. Basically, there are things that need to be done." Grace ended the discussion promptly, not willing for it to enter dangerous waters. Hailey understood what she did and followed through with it.

"I guess I know what you mean. Let me take Jade a beer. See you around." Hailey said with a tone of finality, leaving Grace to her own devices. Grace was grateful for that as she just nodded her head and watched Hailey walk away. Her thoughts were muddled up beyond comprehension.

Chapter Three

The next day, Grace was getting ready to perform with her band, and she flipped through a couple of pages of notes, tuning her violin as she worked. She shook her head once. The image of Hailey's face and the smile she had come unbidden into her head. The fiery gaze that she couldn't forget, no matter how much she tried. She didn't like it, she didn't like it at all. It was something she didn't want to explore, not knowing how devastating the repercussions would be. It was a thought better left unattended. She returned to tuning her violin and humming slowly to herself.

Jade was wearing navy blue overalls, sitting on the table in front of an electricity box at work. She looked totally bored and her environment wasn't helping matters. She absently took bites from a burger while texting to a group on her mobile phone. A builder walked by, carrying a ladder. Some other builders are having tea and talking to each other. She was oblivious to everything else. Her text read;

"Guys, fancy getting together after work for a coffee and cannoli at an Italian café? Confirm and I'll send you the link. :)"

She sat and waited, taking another bite out of her burger again.

Grace was in a dilemma. She was in bed, reading a novel. It was a pretty good one but she found herself unable to concentrate on a single word. The words flew past her head and tried as she did, she couldn't make sense of it. She had a stupid grin on her face that definitely didn't come from the book she wasn't concentrating on. After trying and failing a few times, she placed the book on her chest and stared at the ceiling, thoughts swirling in her head. She couldn't concentrate because of what happened the day before. Whenever she tried to think of something else, the images of Hailey came unbidden to her.

The sky was darkening, showing signs of the night. Grace knew that it was already becoming late but she had stuff to do. The party was over and Jade was collecting a couple of glasses strewn about the garden. The garden was messy so she was trying her best to put it all in order. She was carrying the glasses back to the kitchen.

"I'll join you in a sec," Jade said as she walked back to the kitchen, cradling a couple of glasses in her hands in order for them not to break.

"See you soon," Hailey said softly to Grace as soon as Jade was out of earshot, sharing a look that Grace couldn't decipher. She pulled Grace into a hug which Grace reciprocated.

Grace stumbled out of her reverie with a groan of frustration. She couldn't even sleep well!

***

Grace took a sip of her coffee after she already decided to rendezvous with Jade after the text message was sent out. She sat next to the couple, who were looking at the menu. After that, they became engrossed in each other. She watched as Jade and Hailey, the couple, locked lips and rolled her eyes, turning to the only other girl there aside from the lovebirds. Lucy was a tiny girl with big happy eyes. She wore a flowery shirt and a short skirt on that day. She was sitting next to Jade in front of Grace. Grace decided to strike up a conversation with Lucy.

"This area has come a long way. There's always something going on, and the cafés and restaurants have such a great atmosphere." Grace kickstarted the conversation and Lucy was happy to have someone to talk to seeing as Jade and Hailey were busy with each other.

"Yeah, I remember they used to say it was the neighborhood god had forgotten. So many crimes used to happen every day." She said with gusto, returning the same energy Grace brought to the conversation.

While the two were talking, Jade broke away from her kiss and stole everyone's attention by pointing at a cannoli.

"Guys! Try these fabulous Sicilian ricotta cheese cannoli. Seriously, these are the best around." The excitement in her voice was enough to convince anyone and Lucy was the first to voice it.

"I trust you. Let me try one and I'll give you my honest feedback." Jade was happy to hear Lucy's comment and she reclined on the chair, contentment written all over her face and gestures.

"I have to go to the bathroom. I'll be back." Hailey said to the group, more to Grace's benefit who she was trying so hard not to stare at. She kissed Jade on the cheeks and made her way to the bathroom.

Hailey walked into the bathroom and headed straight for

the mirror, staring at herself. She bit her lips a little, ran a finger or two into her hair, and made sure it was properly messy. She sighed audibly. She didn't know exactly what she was doing or what the point was. But she knew that she had to do it anyway.

She walked back to the group after taking a few minutes to compose herself. She finds the other four in a heated conversation and Grace looking out of place. Lucy engaged Jade and the other two so she didn't have to do much to steal Grace's attention. She grabbed a chair and sat astride it, putting it at a 45-degree angle, facing Grace. She spoke loudly to get Grace's full attention. Not like the others would notice, seeing how engrossed they were in their argument.

"I wanted to surprise Jade by taking her to the light event this weekend. I was going to ask you to join us if you like?" Hailey asked Grace who didn't bother to hide her smile. It was a tricky question.

"Where is that and what is it exactly?" Grace asked, genuinely curious. Hailey Didn't waste time. She pulled out her mobile phone and held it close to Grace's face, showing her the event information.

"Basically, there is an artist who creates concepts using lights and neon," Hailey explained to Grace but Grace already readied herself to decline. Hailey was doing things to her body she couldn't understand. The images of her assaulting Grace's vision were enough to prove that Hailey was dangerous to her peace of mind.

"I'm not sure it's the kind of thing I would be interested in. Thanks anyway, but I'm sure Jade would love it." Grace replied, deftly evading the question and bringing the discussion back to Jade. She didn't know what Hailey's play was but her eyes lingered a little too long on Hailey's messy hair and pouty lips. She knew then that she was a goner. More or less.

"How do you like to be surprised?" Hailey threw the question out there and Grace was taken aback for a sec. She'd not thought about it in a while.

"A bunch of tulips in different colors, I guess! How about you?" Grace replied after deliberating for a while. She then answered as sincerely as she could, betraying nothing.

Jade kept looking over at them, just nodding along to the conversation with the couple. She wasn't concentrating on the argument anymore. The chemistry between Grace and Hailey Could be spotted from a mile away. She didn't like what she was seeing, not by a long shot.

"What about you? What counts as a surprise for you?" Grace found herself asking, irresistibly pulled to Hailey In a way she couldn't explain.

"A girl that I love takes me to a random dark jazz bar. After a couple of espresso martinis, she whispers in my ear that she hasn't stopped thinking about me since she met me." Hailey replied, turning her voice into a whisper as she stared into Grace's eyes while she spoke, the moment becoming suddenly heated.

Jade hated that. There was no way she could tolerate her girlfriend flirting with another woman while she was in the room. Of course, Hailey was her own person; obstinately so. But still, she didn't like what was going on right in front of her. She raised her voice to remind Hailey of the engagement she had planned earlier that day.

"Hailey, didn't you say that you want to see your friend later on tonight?" Jade raised her voice enough to be heard over their private discussion.

Hailey and Grace both look at Jade. Hailey looks startled, as though waking up from an all too pleasant dream.

"Oh… yes." She said as though she'd only just remembered. Jade watched the scene in front of her with mixed feelings.

"Let's get coffee sometime?" Hailey turned to Grace, throwing the question at her. Grace didn't know where it was all going but she knew that she was being pulled in a direction that there'd be no going back from. She decided that she didn't mind, one bit.

"Sure, why not?" She replied as Hailey smiled at her in acknowledgment and said goodbye to everyone before she made her way out of the coffee shop.

Jade was fuming. She decided to indirectly confront Grace in the guise of sarcasm. Although her words were dripping with venom. She decided to interrogate Grace and see what she was hiding.

"Now you wanna have coffee with my girlfriend, huh?" Jade asked, not bothering to mask the hysterical edge to her voice. Either Grace didn't notice or she was smart enough to ignore it.

"Don't be silly! She wanted to surprise you by taking you

somewhere, she wanted to know if it was something you would like." Grace replied, and Jade stared at her for a few seconds before nodding and going about her business.

Chapter Four

It was afternoon, Grace was in her living room. She drew one of the four sets of curtains in her living room. Tom was there, seated on a chair. He took a sip from the drink he held in one hand.

"Are you going to tell me what exactly happened that made you leave everything behind?" Tom asked, not bothering to beat about the bush. He noticed that Grace was avoiding having a discussion and she did everything else but actually talk.

"I guess I have to tell someone." She said, walking to another curtain and drawing it up. The room became brighter. She heaved a breath as she began to think of what transpired between her and Hailey.

Hailey fixed her apron before making a coffee for a waiting customer. She smiled when she gave a coffee to the customer. She looked distracted, checking the clock. Finally, she grabbed her phone and sent a text to Grace, unable to keep still. The events that had transpired between them made her unable to sit still. She found herself jittery with nerves like a schoolgirl during Prom. Her text read:

"Morning Grace! Just wanted to say thanks for the lovely conversations! And also hope to see you soon. x"

She threw her phone as anxiety overcame her body and almost instantly regretted sending the text. She didn't know how Grace was going to take it and she wondered how much damage a single text could cause.

Grace laid on her bed that night, a soft jazz song coming from the speakers. It was Melody Gardot again. She was reading Hailey's text over and over again as butterflies danced in her stomach.

"They say the poisoned vine breeds a finer wine"

The lyrics of the song stood out for Grace, seeing as whatever she wished to have with Hailey was morally unacceptable. But, she couldn't help it. That was the main reason she never sent a text back. She didn't want to fan the flames she didn't understand.

***

Grace walked to the building's entrance. She is texting someone.

"Tennis?"

She sent a message and waited for a reply. In a few seconds, she got one. It was from Jade.

"Would love to but I'm off to the hospital. feeling pain since noon. I'm guessing it's that damn kidney stone again."

Grace felt concerned for her friend as she hurriedly began to make her way to Jade's place.

"I'll drive you, be there in 20 minutes."

She turned back from the building, walking towards her car as fast as she could. A kidney stone could be deadly sometimes. She didn't bother trying to think too much about it, she gunned the engine and was out of there in a flash. Her heart racing erratically in her chest, she drove even faster, worrying about tying her chest in knots, hoping that she wasn't too late.

When she arrived at Jade's, she parked the car and simultaneously killed the engine, not bothering to stay even a second more. There was no need for words seeing as Jade was already waiting. She was grimacing in pain which worried Grace. But she said nothing and Grace didn't bother to try to bring up a conversation. They drove in silence up to the hospital.

Jade talked to a receptionist at the counter. It was all hush-hush. Grace was standing behind her, not willing to move forward to listen to the conversation. It rubbed her wrong somehow. After the receptionist showed Jade where to go, Grace followed. They walked to the waiting room and they sat on two of the available seats, lost in thoughts. Small talks weren't needed.

Grace picked up some papers and a pen from her bag while she was sitting next to Jade in A & E. Jade remained silent so Grace focused on something else. The air around them was brittle with tension and she didn't understand it. She fiddled with her pen and opened a page. She started reading it, leaving Jade to her devices. Jade preferred it that way seeing as she did nothing to bridge whatever gap was between them. She took out her mobile phone and began to play with it, just fiddling with no exact destination. While she was doing that, her phone rang, startling her. Even Grace was startled although she masked it pretty well. She knew who was calling from the way Jade's face changed into one of pure adoration. She wondered if someone would ever think of her like that.

"Yes, baby... I don't know, it was at noon when the pain started... Grace is here... yeah, she came to pick me up. Okay, darling... sure, see you then."

Jade hung up the phone and didn't bother to say anything to Grace. Grace did the same, fiddling with her pen. She sensed that something was wrong but she didn't have any proof so she went back to what she was doing. Thankfully, Jade resumed playing with her phone again.

"Do you want a coffee or something?" Grace asked, after realizing that the silence was choking. She decided to damn it all to hell and extend a hand of peace.

"Nah, thanks." Jade didn't even bother to look at her, which made Grace shrug, after deciding that she'd done her best and she left the rest up to fate to help her handle. She didn't know what was wrong but she decided to stop pushing it for the time being. At least, until Jade was feeling up to telling her.

The hospital hallway was quiet as Grace's shoes made cobbling sounds while she walked down the hallway to the place where the vending machine was. She inserted a few coins in the vending machine and chose her coffee. She liked it black, especially when she had a lot of thoughts muddling her head.

She looked at her wristwatch and stretched her body.
She gave a yawn of exhaustion, flexing her fingers.
She waited for the coffee to be ready and she
grabbed it and walked back to the waiting room. She wondered if she'd see Jade in a better mood. She hoped so at least.

Grace picked up her papers from the seat in order to sit down; she sipped her coffee, and placing the cup on the floor next to her seat. She stared at Jade who remained oblivious to her before she decided to go back to what she was reading. Jade was scrolling down her Facebook page on her mobile, checking out posts and making comments. After a few moments though, she turned to Grace who was engrossed in what she was reading and not even realizing that Jade was there. Jade envied it somewhat. Grace could zone out of everything.

"*What are you reading?*" *Jade asked, honestly curious. She was bridling with curiosity even though she kept it under lock and key. But something about that moment was different, even though she couldn't place it.*

"*How to control things when they're getting out of control.*" *Grace replied, not missing a beat. She didn't even turn to look at Jade. Jade was peeved, wondering if maybe she could have been there with someone else instead of Grace.*

Jade just harrumphed and left her to it. She kept fiddling with her phone and Grace kept reading. Something nudged Grace to look up though and she couldn't help the smile that morphed onto her face as she looked up to see Hailey walking towards them. Hailey was even more beautiful than she had remembered and tried as she did to get the thoughts out of her head, but she couldn't. Thankfully, a nurse called Jade's name, startling Grace out of her reverie, of which she was grateful for. She didn't want thoughts of Hailey fiddling with her thoughts any more than necessary. Jade saw Hailey and her face lit up. She stood up abruptly and grabbed Hailey Into a hug. She planted a couple of kisses on Hailey's lips and turned to the nurse who gestured for her to walk through the door after washing her hand with sanitizer liquid. She did as she was told though, no questions asked. Although she left Grace back in the waiting room. Thankfully, Hailey Returned to the waiting room and took the seat where Jade was. Grace could feel herself becoming even more self-conscious and somehow, she didn't like it. Hailey was doing things to her.

Grace and Hailey were in the waiting room, none of them actually speaking first even though it was clear that they both wanted to converse with each other.

"*How's your day been? You look tired.*" *Grace decided to pick up the conversation and see where it was going to lead from there. She didn't fool herself to believe that something was going to happen between her* and Hailey, not in the least.

"I haven't been getting enough sleep these days," Hailey replied and Grace could see the signs all over her. It was in the eye-bags underneath her eyes, even though it did nothing to diminish her appeal. Grace felt concerned, seeing Hailey in such a state.

"You should have gone home to sleep, I'd take care of Jade." She said, trying to restrain herself from stretching out her hands to touch Hailey's face. It was a pretty hard thing to do.

"I came to see you, too," Hailey said sincerely and Grace felt a warmth pool up between her legs. It was embarrassing, the kind of thoughts she was having about someone who was already taken, but she couldn't help herself. And she hated herself for that.

Hailey Averted her gaze, trying to look anywhere else. She knew what she was doing was wrong but she couldn't help herself too. Grace blushed, unable to say a word.

"Tell me about that light event. How was it?" Grace asked, finding herself unable to stare away from Hailey. Hailey was exotic in ways she couldn't explain. In a way, she didn't want to. It was ecstasy, it was bliss. It was everything she wanted but didn't have. And that was the saddest part.

Chapter Five

Grace put wood on the fire. She didn't add the last log in her hand and turned back to Tom after she finished telling him about what had transpired between her and the girls. Thankfully, he was a good listener. She stared at the flames while she talked, unable to stare at him. It was difficult, knowing that someone was pining over you and you were pining over someone else.

"We had our moments, you know?" She said after a brief pause, deciding to damn it all and bare it out.

"Didn't you want more?" Tom asked, staring at Grace. He could tell that there was a lot on her mind she wasn't sharing and he planned to do whatever he could to bring it all out to the surface.

Grace grabbed a poker to prod the fire, making space for the last log. The fire sparked, and she moved her head away. She was doing it in a routine way, just moving her fingers to keep herself busy.

"Have you ever seen yourself from a third person perspective? That's who I was at the time. I was blaming myself and then again, at the same time, I let myself enjoy it." She spoke, her words carrying more weight than she intended. She had another flashback.

Jade went to the toilet, leaving Hailey And Grace alone. After Hailey realized that she was alone with Grace, she narrowed her eyes with desire and whispered;

"SIP IT." Her voice came out more sultry than she intended, bowling Grace over with just how suggestive it was. Grace didn't think she was that bold but Hailey's eyes suggested something different. Grace decided to play the game and see where it would lead.

Hailey offered her whiskey to Grace and she took the glass gracefully, gazing at Hailey. She stared at Hailey a little longer than necessary, trying to convey her longing without using words. It was difficult. She decided to down the drink instead. She made a disgusted face, as the drink was bitter, even more bitter than she had expected. Hailey giggled, as though she'd found some sort of entertainment and finally offered her a glass of water, of which she was grateful for. She downed it all in one gulp and sighed a breath of contentment. Hailey just watched, a smile dancing on her face.

"Have you ever asked yourself what is missing from that perfect picture of your life?" Grace asked Hailey, thinking about the events of the past few days and how she'd bridge the gap. It wasn't an easy thing to do. It was hard actually, going by the way she wanted to phrase her sentences in such a way that they wouldn't seem suspicious.

"Hmmm." Hailey replied, not saying anything else. Grace could see that she was thinking about something even though she didn't know what. But she only hoped it was along the lines of what she was thinking about.

Before Hailey could give a coherent reply though, Jade got back to the table. She narrowed her eyes slightly at Hailey and Grace who were sitting still, not saying a word. She suspected that they must have been talking but stopped when she arrived. That's what made it even more suspicious. Grace saw Jade's gaze and decided to clear the air before she was misconstrued.

"We were talking about what is missing in our lives." Grace said to Jade, who stared at Hailey. She didn't say a word at first, just looked as lost in thoughts as Hailey was. Grace realized that they probably hadn't examined that question at all.

Hailey looked at Jade, deciding to find out the answer from Jade and wondering if she was missing anything. She decided to say it anyway. She didn't understand who she was anymore and needed clarity on the subject.

"I really wanna know your answer to this." Hailey more or less pleaded with Jade, her eyes doing the pleading. Jade stared at her for a second and decided to just answer it as she deemed fit. It didn't seem all that important to her but she could tell it was important to Hailey. So, she answered.

"Well... I guess I will buy my own apartment and be self-employed." Her reply sounded mundane even to her ears but surprisingly, she realized that that's what she wanted. To own a place of her own and be her own boss. Nobody roused her from sleep until she was ready. It seemed like such a blissful way to live. Saddening that she didn't have that though.

Hailey didn't get the response she wanted from Jade so, she just nodded her head carelessly. Her mind was still muddled up. She hadn't put much thought to it before and somehow, that grated on her nerves. Grace could tell she'd struck gold so she took another sip of her wine and watched it all unfold.

"And of course what's missing changes at every stage in your life. It is not the same as it was ten years ago, or what it will be in the future." Grace replied conversationally, realizing that her questions would give Hailey and Jade something to think about for a while. She'd always been intrigued by the concept of people being people. People growing and learning from their past mistakes and heading forward into a future. Although there'll be mistakes, it'll be worth it anyways.

After that, there wasn't much conversation. It was just the way Grace envisioned it. Jade was lost in thought and Hailey kept stealing glances at her whenever she felt she could get away with it. Hailey leaned on Jade's shoulders and stared at Grace, her eyes conveying the things her mouth couldn't say.

***

It was closing time at the coffee shop that Hailey worked in. She was listening to Clare Teal's song on her mobile, on speaker, and cleaning the coffee machine. Her thoughts kept going back to Grace and the conversation they had. She found herself restless in more ways than one.

"Well there's some high and mighty people
In this big judgmental world."

Clare Teal's voice lended credence to her thoughts. She suddenly grabbed her mobile and shared the song to Grace by text. She didn't want to have to listen to it alone and somehow, she felt like Grace would understand where she was coming from.

Grace walked towards the bus station; she had a violin case in her hand. She was carefree as usual but then, something was different. She didn't know what. A few seconds later, she found out what it was. She noticed a text message from Hailey Sending her a song. She hadn't listened to it before even though she was a big fan of music. Hailey's sharing that song made her feel excited. She couldn't wait to listen.

When she got to the station, she put on her headphones and played the song that Haileyhad just sent. It was more beautiful than she anticipated. The song carried on, transporting her into another world, another realm...

> *"Well, you told me lots of stories*
> *You said look but do not touch*
> *Well, babe, we all do things we don't admire*
> *So don't sit there and plead with me*
> *Just hush your mouth, take heed of me*
> *Cause everybody's messin' with fire."*

It was a song by an artist Grace didn't recognize but she loved it nonetheless. She remembered Hailey's smile and the moment she offered her whiskey, narrowing her eyes and saying 'sip it.' That was the highlight of her day, seeing how audacious Hailey had become.

The sound of 'sip it' fades into the line 'messin' with fire.

Grace looked Tom in the eye, her flashback coming to an end. It was a pretty crazy thing, realizing that she was talking to Tom about such sensitive things and not feeling self conscious about it. She decided that maybe she was too hard on him and finding a common ground was what she actually needed to do.

"Have you watched Claire's Knee?" Grace asked Tom who looked totally clueless. She couldn't blame him though, it was not a famous movie, albeit a good one.

"Nah." Tom replied with as much sincerity as he could muster, wondering where she was going with all she was saying.

"It's a French movie. The main character wants to touch

Claire's knee for the whole duration of the movie, that's all he wants. But it takes nearly two hours in the movie, and the whole summer holiday, until he does it. In adultery, you experience the extremes of satisfaction and disappointment. Someone always has to suffer but there's joy, too. I just wanted to be with her." Grace replied, more honest with herself than she'd let herself be in a long long while. It would have been refreshing if it wasn't so downright painful. She felt another flashback coming on and this time, she didn't fight it. In fact, she let herself be led by it.

Chapter Six

Hailey walked towards Grace, her steps slow and quiet, not alerting Grace to her presence which was the way she liked it. She wanted to surprise her, not startle her but give her a mild feeling that would rush through body. Grace wasn't expecting it, she wasn't expecting anything or anyone. She was smoking alone, puffing into the air. There was one else around so there was nobody to berate her for it, to tell her it wasn't right. "Don't you know smoking is bad for your health," they would say. She hated it.

"Can I have a drag?"

Hailey came up to her and Grace raised her head to see her just standing there. Her mind went blank for a minute, but colorful thoughts soon started to mushroom within her. Grace smiled when she saw the deep, welcoming gaze of Hailey, and her bright smile fixed on her. Grace smiled as well, and the atmosphere around them changed. The two wouldn't care if it was stormy outside, their warmth that day was enough. The day was about to set, to come to an end, and the mere fact that they were all alone gave an intimate feel to it.

"Sure." Grace replied. She was ready to play with fire that night. To bear it all, to let the fires of her passion consume her. And damn it all to hell the next day.

Hailey grabbed the cigarette and took a step towards Grace, she wore a sly smile looking into Grace's expectant eyes. Grace didn't know what she was up to, but she waited and watched. Hailey brought the cigarette to her red lips and drew at it, the end of the cigarette glowed a dim orange light.

Grace's eyes squinted as she waved off smoke from her face, laughing and moving away from Hailey. Hailey started cackling heartily as Grace moved back, her back bent and her right arm across her stomach in a laugh. She had blown the puffy smoke from the cigarette into Grace's face, a joke she thought would make them both laugh. She was right, it did make them laugh. Grace especially, and Hailey's skin was flushed with ambient emotions.

"Come on, now, you didn't have to do that," Grace said. She was no longer waving smoke off her face, her eyes no longer burned, and she wasn't gasping for air anymore. But, above all of that, Grace's heart beated in a rhythm that made her feel as light as air.

A moment later, when the cackling had stopped, and the two ladies stood side by side, Hailey gazed at Grace's pouting lips, its plump lower half drawing her in the more she stared. Grace's lips looked too good and Hailey couldn't help herself.

She found herself leaning forward and kissing Grace's lips. It happened so sudden, too sudden for her to stop herself. But, it was late. Too late. Hailey threw caution to the wind and rode the waves of the euphoria rushing through her like a sea of molten lava.

The sea burned even fiercer as Grace reciprocated with the same fervor. Grace kissed back passionately, her hands reaching up to curl themselves into Hailey's hair. Hailey dropped the cigarette, putting it out with the heel of her shoes. She placed her fingers gently on Grace's face and lost herself in Grace's arms. There was no need for words, they'd had enough words to last a lifetime.

All they wanted was to feel each other and drown in the moment. They kissed each other with a burning sensation of love and passion, unable to pull away from themselves. It'd been a long time coming and this time, Grace decided that she was going to go ahead with it, no secrets whatsoever. No looking back. To damn it all to hell.

Grace broke away from the kiss, "my place?" Grace asked, staring into Hailey's misty eyes. They were stormy with arousal, and Grace realized that no words were needed for what they were about to do. She held Hailey and led her into her house. It was a slow process, one they were willing to take their time.

They wanted each other. There was no higher reason for not wanting it. After that day Grace met Hailey, she'd not been sane enough to take steps to stay away from her. She tried though, she really did. Yet, she was always pulled back to the thoughts of Hailey and none of those thoughts were innocent. Not even one. She suspected that she was going to be miserable after everything but she just wanted one single night where she could be wild and totally free. With Hailey beside her.

As they got to the door, there wasn't a moment's delay as they locked their lips in a passionate, wet kiss, unable to put their hands off each other. They couldn't, and they loved it. Grace felt Hailey's hands slide down to her breasts and she moaned in pleasure as she felt a tingling sensation flush through her entire body. It only made her want Hailey more, and likewise, Hailey felt the same.

Grace was wearing a turtleneck and a pair of trousers which annoyed her to no end. If she'd known Hailey was coming, she would have definitely worn something that suited the moment. Something like a gown, perhaps. But then, there was no time to cry over spilt milk. She made a sign for Hailey to wait while she undressed herself. Hailey obliged. Hailey was wearing a flimsy gown that left nothing to the imagination. She wore panties though but her nipples were hardening and they perked up in her dress. Grace could see those nipples, and she imagined how it would feel in her mouth. She got shivers thinking about it.

Grace removed the turtleneck first, wearing only a camisole. Her pants followed, bringing her black lacy panties into view. Hailey licked her lips as she stared, her skin burning with passion for Grace. She was endowed in all the right places. Now only in her black panties and camisole, Grace moved toward Hailey who was seated on the couch.

"I'll relieve you of this." Grace said to Hailey, pulling at her shirt as she made to take it off her.

Hailey smiled. She loved that Grace was taking off her clothes, her hands brushing against her skin. For some reason, it felt wrong to break the moment with words of gratitude. So, she didn't say anything, she let herself be led by Grace.

Grace took off the shirt, taking her time to stare at Hailey's alluring body. How it had always assaulted her dreams and made a mess of her life in more ways than one. The same body that made her unable to concentrate, causing her mind to drift off so very often. Staring at that body, the smoothness of it, filled her with a sense of fulfillment she couldn't place. And here she was, about to have a feel of it, to touch it, to have it pressed against hers. Grace salivated at the thought of it.

"You're beautiful." She muttered, her breath hitching in her throat. She couldn't say the words without her voice breaking up.

"So, are you," Hailey whispered.

Grace wanted her hands all over Hailey, wanted to let Hailey know how much she'd craved for this moment. She was almost shaking, holding herself together. She wanted Hailey's soft hands on her, on her breasts again. But before that, she wanted to let Hailey feel everything she'd envisioned, not a single thing will be left out.

Hailey was even shyer than she expected, which put Grace in the lead. She wanted to show Hailey what loving someone was like. What proving it without words was like. Grace wanted this moment to be memorable for her, for Hailey.

Grace took her time undressing Hailey, her eyes caressing Hailey's body. She was still in a camisole and panties whereas Hailey had just a flimsy gown on. She used her fingers to remove the strap of the gown off Hailey's shoulders, the moment becoming even more intimate as Grace got fully into it. She couldn't be stopped at that point. Hailey didn't even think about stopping her. It was everything she wanted and more.

Her gown pooled at her feet as her perky nipples became exposed to the air. They got even perkier as she felt the warmth of Grace. Grace stepped back to admire Hailey's body, her small, perky breasts, her slim build, her curved hips. It aroused her as she stared, then, she removed her camisole in one fell swoop. Hailey could see her mouth hanging open but she couldn't help it. Grace's breasts were unlike anything she had seen, full and round, and the lights inside made it shine even more. It made Hailey's eyes bound even harder.

"You like what you see?" Grace noticed how Hailey was gawking at her. Hailey looked up, into Grace's eyes, she nodded a reply, completely bowled over by Grace's beauty.

She decided to not let Grace do the dominating so she walked up to Grace, her breasts pressed against Grace's. 'Oh, the feeling,' Hailey thought.

Her eyes still fixed on Grace, she began to slowly remove Grace's panties, her thumb brushing against Grace's bare, brown skin. Soon, she let them fall to the floor. Grace felt left out, so she did the same. Slower, with more passion, not taking her eyes away from Hailey's gaze.

They stood before each other, naked and pulsing with desire. A desire for their bodies. it was in the air all around them. They could sense it, breathe it in, even taste it. And they could see it in each other's eyes, drowning themselves in the sea of emotions. A good kind of drowning.

At first, Hailey never intended to go all the way with Grace. When she met Grace at Jade's birthday party, she could remember just admiring her individuality from afar. But after they spoke, Grace was stuck in her mind. She had to keep seeing her anytime they hung out. It was torture, the worst kind. To crave something right in front of you, yet, you are unable to touch it. It was indeed torture.

Grace felt the same, seeing Hailey in her dreams most nights. Even when she zones out, Hailey's face comes unbidden to her. She felt assaulted by it. With Hailey now beside her, Grace was going to let herself run wild.

Hailey placed a soulful kiss on Grace, a meshing of tongues and lips as their bodies brushed against each other. Their bodies were screaming with pleasure. They devoured each other as they sucked on their lips, their eyes closed and their breath warm and stiff. Grace pushed Hailey onto a sofa as her tongue danced in her mouth. Hailey gave out a moan, her breath coming in ragged gasps.

Grace broke up the kiss, and placed it on Hailey's neck in soft kisses that sent a rush through Hailey's body. She'd never imagined that she could feel a mix of emotions so strongly that she'd feel like she was in another reality. A blissful reality. Grace did her job dutifully, making Hailey writhe in pleasure that made her quiver. Grace could feel her trembling.

Her lips and tongue caressed the upper side of Hailey's breasts as Hailey sucked in a breath. She was shocked that Grace was so bold. So audacious. So beautiful. So hot. She was panting, her body craving Grace even greater. She didn't spare Hailey for one minuscule second.

When her lips finally found a way to Hailey's nipples, Hailey gasped as she felt her nipples explode with pleasure. The feeling of Grace's warm lips closing in on her nipples sent a wave through her unlike any other she'd ever experienced. She screamed out loud at the sheer craziness of it all. It was wild. It was untamed. It was precisely what she wanted, what she needed. She was unapologetic about it now.

Grace's tongue played with Hailey's nipples in ways she had never done before, playing with them as though they were made for that very reason. For Grace, time stopped, only the air moved. Everything else didn't matter at that point. Not Jade. Not the repercussions. Nothing!

Only Hailey's naked body lying under her mattered. She didn't let herself think of anything else. She was glad Hailey made the first move because she wasn't sure she could. And she loved it.

She planted light kisses on Hailey's breasts. The arch of Hailey's back after she did that made her smile, knowing that she was doing something right. She went at it again with renewed vigor but Hailey got her senses back. In those few moments, Hailey moved to pleasure Grace. She took a look at Grace and said;

"It's my turn. Don't be greedy, would you?"

Grace could see the lust burning in her eyes and something else. Something she was scared to name. Grace let her body go supple, taking Hailey's position, and Hailey took the place she did. Hailey felt suddenly powerful, having Grace underneath her like that.

She placed a kiss on Grace's nose. Then, she began to use her lips, teeth and tongue to show Grace how much she appreciated all she had done to her that night.

Grace took in a breath, surprised to find out that one mouth could make her feel so much. When Hailey lightly nibbled on her ears, she knew she was a goner. The moans that came from her lips sounded alien to her. It sounded so wild and feral, it was so unlike her. She felt uninhibited, free. It was a feeling she'd craved for so long and it felt so fulfilling.

Hailey let herself lead, her heart pounding to the moans from Grace. It excited her actually, hearing Grace make those sounds. It drove her to pleasure Grace more. She felt proud of herself, and wanted to soak in all the goodness from the temple beneath her.

She let her tongue roam, coursing through Grace's ample cleavage. She licked, kissed, bit, and sucked wherever her mouth laid, with Grace's moans pushing her forward. She decided to kick it up a notch and decided that Grace was to be blamed for her wildness that night.

She held Grace's breasts and gave them a squeeze, covering her mouth over the two perky nipples. Grace screamed and moaned at the same time, bucking her hips and arching her back, her gaze raised to the ceiling. Hailey smiled within her as she took away her lips from Grace's nipples, using her teeth to bite lightly on them. Grace was going mad as she shook, and Hailey decided that she was going to put her out of her misery, though not yet. She still needed to play a little bit more.

She used her fingers to draw circles on Grace's abdomen while her mouth remained busy on Grace's breasts. Every single movement she made, Grace jerked in response. Her body was becoming so sensitive, she could feel so many things happen to her at once. It was something she hadn't felt before, something she wasn't sure she'd ever let herself feel.

Her body was on fire. It was burning, and she was losing herself. Her mind was thoughtless. There was so much going on that she couldn't place, so much. She loved it. She loved the feeling as it consumed her whole. She couldn't remember the last time she felt so whole, so at peace with herself. She couldn't remember the last time she actually felt alive.

At that moment, she was more awake than ever. Soaring over the clouds. At that moment, she could do anything and there was nobody on the earth that could stop her.

Hailey could feel the very same thing Grace felt, and she wondered why she'd not felt it before. Even with all she had going with Jade, she hadn't felt so much from a single person in a very long time. Her fingers moved before her mind did, her tongue flickered before she asked it to. Her body led and she followed.

"Let's take this to the bedroom." Grace muttered as she tried to catch her breath and Hailey seconded. She couldn't wait to feel that wildness in her again.

"Lead the way." Hailey said, and Grace did, holding Hailey's hand, not daring to look back in case it was a spell that could be broken.

Here was a moment of two women in an intense embrace, as both moved and slid their nude bodies against each other in bed. There was a recklessness to their lovemaking, it was beautiful how they were intertwined in such a way that any heart would quake at the sight. There was wildness, and the night was tranquil enough to conceal it. The both of them were going mad as they dove into themselves.

There was something different about it, it wasn't practiced or planned. It just happened. Their bodies lead them where they should follow. There were no words. There wasn't any need for one. At that moment, they were the only ones who existed in the world. It was like one moment extended into eternity.

After a wild night of forbidden passion, Grace with her black silky hair was very visible between the white sheets. She emerged from a deep sleep, groggily. She moved the sheets aside and looked frustrated when she found herself alone in the bed. She moved her hand down to her body, between her legs, jerking and spasming. But it felt unnatural somehow, forced even. It was so unsettling for her and she cried out, unable to believe that she had to make do with such an excuse of an orgasm. She turned her head to the side, closed her eyes and slept off again.

Grace and Hailey were playing the violin naked in front of each other. There was a tranquility in the air as the two played without regards for modesty. They gazed into each other's eyes, the music saying the words they couldn't say. The violin playing intensified in tension as the music grew into a crescendo. Hailey practically hammered the bow on the violin's arch. Jade came out of nowhere and kissed Hailey's lips. Grace felt white hot rage fuel her body and avert her gaze and stopped playing with a cold smile on her face.

The moonlight gave way to the sunshine of the next morning. It was a new day.

Chapter Seven

Grace drove towards the coffee-shop where Hailey worked. She tried talking herself out of it but it was a losing game. Her brain wasn't thinking anymore. In fact, she wasn't sure she could stop herself from going there even if she held a gun to her head. That was how bad it was, seeing Hailey in her dream like that. She slowed down as soon as she got within range, heart hammering in her chest. She could tell it was a bad idea but she couldn't stop herself. Her mind was screaming and danger signs flashed in her subconscious.

She looked and saw what her subconscious was warning her about. Hailey and Jade were having coffee in paper cups in front of the shop. Hailey was giggling. They shared a cigarette together. Grace felt a white hot rage bubbling from within as she floored the accelerator and hightailed it out of there, hoping she wasn't seen by either of the two. Her heart hammered in her chest in a painful rhythm.

She drove even faster, her eyes glued to the endless road in front of her. She turned up the volume of her music, hoping that she'd be able to drown the sound of her heartbeat. Her face turned pale as she stared at the front mirror. She looked as though she aged ten years in a single morning. Her hand shook on the wheel and even the music did nothing to save her at that point. In her opinion, nothing else mattered. So, she drove and drowned out the sound of everything else.

Grace had gotten home that evening and was drinking whiskey. Her eyes were slowly becoming blurry as she stared at the bottle in front of her. The bottle was half empty as she'd downed almost half in a single gulp. It burned a trail down her throat and it reminded her of the pain that assaulted her mind when she saw Jade and Hailey.

It came unbidden to her and tried as she did, she couldn't forget. She smoked a cigarette, puffing into the air. The nostalgia of the time she had with Hailey's teasing was catching up with her but she didn't pay it any mind. The TV was on but she didn't pay it any attention. She lay down to smoke, watching the tendrils of smoke form circles that dispersed in the air. She placed her left hand on her forehead, massaging it. She sat up and tapped the ashes into an ashtray which was beyond her reach. The doorbell rings. She was so startled, it took her a moment to get her bearings. She stared at the clock. It was late. She turned towards the sound.

She stood up and went to check the peephole. Hailey was standing behind the door, looking stressed out. Grace's heart went out to her almost immediately. Even with what happened earlier that day, her heart wasn't strong enough to just turn Hailey away. She immediately opened the door, trying to keep her face in a mask of calmness.

Hailey threw herself into Grace's arms and shut the door with her foot. She didn't bother with pleasantries which was the way Grace liked it. They kissed passionately; Grace pushed Hailey Up against the wall. Grace couldn't believe it was genuinely happening. After the too realistic dreams she had, she wanted Hailey even more than ever. She moved her hand up under Hailey's shirt. Hailey moaned and sighed as soon as Grace's hand touched her skin. Hailey kissed Grace intensely and ran her hands through Grace's hair.

Hailey's mobile rings; she ignored it. Grace stopped. Everything felt wrong. Hailey was in a relationship with her friend, she had no business with her. Grace takes a step back, trying to collect her bearings. She rubbed her lips with her thumb, hung her head for a second then gazed at Hailey, wondering how exactly she came to be in such a situation.

"This isn't right." Grace said, always the voice of reason. She realized that a dream was just that—a dream. But if she crossed the threshold she was about to, then she was genuinely going to cross boundaries.

"But it feels just right." Hailey said, tiredness coming off her in waves. Grace could sympathize with her predicament, she was conflicted too. But then, Hailey was her friend's girlfriend. She didn't want to be a bad friend.

Hailey sat there, against the wall, holding her head in her hands. Grace didn't need a soothsayer to know that Hailey was going through a lot, more than she could say. She decided to thaw the ice, so to speak.

Grace walked to the kitchen, grabbed a glass, wondering if what she was doing was right or hopelessly wrong. She realized that she was going to find out, one way or another.

Grace poured two glasses of whiskey and walked toward the hallway. She hummed to herself as she walked, toying with some scenarios in her head.

The sound of the door closing stopped her in her tracks. She stood still in the middle of the living room, watching the empty place.

Chapter Eight

Grace opened a bottle of red wine as Jade stood next to the fridge.

"I'm here to share some good news with you." Jade said, all smiles.

Grace raised a single eyebrow, wondering what Jade was going on about. There was an intrigue in her words that more or less roused the curiosity in her.

Grace poured two glasses of wine and gave one of them to Jade. She knew that a cause for any of them to celebrate would definitely be a big deal.

"Go ahead." She told Jade who more or less obliged. Although she wasn't expecting what she heard next, she couldn't brace herself for it. The pain that lanced through her body, the ringing in her ears as Jade said the words that she dreaded to hear.

"Hailey is moving in with me next week."

As Jade said the words, Grace felt her world stop. She shook, unable to believe what she was hearing. It hadn't seemed so official until then. She tried to smile and raised her glass in a celebratory gesture. Her hands was still shaking and Jade kept staring at it, not doing anything to disguise the disgust on her face

"I'm happy for you." She said, wondering how she must have sounded. She knew she didn't sound sincere one bit and wondered for a second if Jade picked up on it. In fact, she knew Jade must have known something was wrong. Hailey was too chummy with her. Her hands were shaking again and this time, she couldn't even control them. She felt like she was under water and drowning by the second. It was a sickening feeling.

Jade ignored Grace's glass, which made Grace look at her, skepticism written all over her face. Grace wondered what was coming even though deep down she knew that she wasn't going to go scot-free with the whole fooling around with Hailey thing. She blamed herself, not Hailey. Never Hailey. Hailey probably saw her as an easy picking and turned up the charm, flirting with her while making her feel like she was the most important person in the world. Yet kissing Jade in front of her and expecting her to just take it. Grace couldn't believe how stupid she'd been. It was so dumb, she was tempted to slap herself over the head.

Jade pointedly ignored the look on Grace's and turned back to Grace's fridge and wrote something on the post-it note. She didn't bother to act like she didn't see Grace's hands shaking. That would have been stupid and she knew it. At first, she wanted to believe that Grace and Hailey didn't have anything going on. She wanted to believe it so bad. But then, somehow, they proved her wrong with the guilty looks they sent her way and the lustful look they sent each other's way.

When Grace asked her what she felt was missing from her life, she noticed Grace staring at Hailey in a wistful way. She didn't say anything because it didn't feel like the right time to. That's why the conversation on the table that day felt muted. Because Jade didn't want to admit what she'd known all along. It was hard to pretend, even harder with friends. Jade didn't want to do what she was about to do but then, Grace forced her hand. Jade knew that Hailey loved her, Hailey just liked the thrill of being with somebody else at her back. She decided that she was going to have a long talk with Hailey. But, Grace was different. Grace had been her friend for so long, the betrayal hurt even more at that moment. Maybe that's why she felt anger burning through her like fire through a piece of wood doused with fuel. She wanted Grace to know that she knew what she was up to and didn't like it. She didn't approve one bit. So, she did what she did.

"Are you?" Jade asked, done with the whole pretense. She'd seen how Grace looked at Hailey and it was one too many times to have been an accident. She wasn't the type of person who'd let such a thing go. Never. She was ruthless to a fault sometimes and whenever somebody called her out on it, she pointedly ignored them.

She took a couple of steps forward to stick the paper on Grace's forehead and pushed her wine glass at Grace's chest. She wanted Grace to understand the ramifications of her actions. She and Hailey would definitely trash it out but she wasn't sure she wanted Grace near her or Hailey anymore. Grace was a betrayer in more ways than one and she needed to make a statement to let Grace know that what she did was more or less unpardonable.

Grace felt mortification creep up on her as the ramifications of the situation dawned on her. Jade knew. Jade didn't say a word to suggest she knew but then, her actions proved it. Grace wanted the ground to open up and swallow her alive so she wouldn't have to live with herself and the divide she'd caused her friends. She wished it didn't have to be that way and that she was strong enough to hold back. Even though she didn't go all the way with Hailey, she led her on. She let Hailey do the leading but still. It was all the same. She was trash who didn't deserve her friends.

Grace took a step back and took the glass, steadying her hand. Jade walked away and left the apartment, shutting the door with a loud bang. As the door sounded, so was the sound of her heart breaking. There was this tone of finality to it, a pain that riddled her being

She was scared, she was tired and more than all the others, she felt… dirty. As though she'd committed a crime punishable by death, but death seemed more of a favor than what she was going through at the moment. One would say she was overreacting but she knew she wasn't. She wondered if she'd forgive and forget if she was in Jade's shoes. Probably not.

Grace stood still for a while in silence as she placed the pair of glass cups on the table and kept moving as though she was in a trance. She kept moving forward, going to look at the mirror in the bathroom. She saw herself, with a yellow post-it on her forehead, with the word 'TRAITOR' on it. It was written in big bold letters. Grace felt despair for the first time after a long time.

***

Grace's eyes were red. She rubbed her eyes, staring into space. She couldn't believe how much she'd divulged to Tom and she suddenly became self conscious. More or less. She'd said more than she originally intended. Tom cleaned his glasses, watching her with a blank expression on his face. He didn't know if he'd be able to offer her comfort in any form.

"Thanks for stopping by, but I think you should go now." She said as soon as she realized that she was done talking. She felt like she needed to be alone with her thoughts and having Tom there, although he listened dutifully, wouldn't help matters. She realized that it might have been callous of her but worse would have been leading him on.

Tom looked at Grace, putting his glasses on. He wanted to see her clearly after all she'd said. She looked so fragile, he was tempted to tip her over to see if she'd fold like a pack of cards or break like an egg. None of those prospects were the least bit amusing.

"Let me know if you need—"

"I need to be left alone." She said to Tom, not mincing words.

She saw the look of hurt flash across his face but he masked it before she could mention it. Tom made it as though to talk or offer some form of encouragement but Grace interrupted him mid sentence. She didn't have time to go through with his code of chivalry or whatnots and she wasn't going to pretend. She owed him that much.

She grabbed her violin and began to play as though he was already gone. Tom stood still and watched, looking at Grace as she played a private performance for herself. He sighed and walked out, not wanting to intrude on the moment she'd more or less immortalized. Grace played even more intensely as the door shut behind Tom. She kept playing, her violin giving way to a crescendo that sounded downright heartbroken. She played for her fragile heart, she played for the girl she couldn't have. She played and played, until she was spent. She continued playing still…

***

Grace woke up on the sofa, drenched in sweat. She looked at the clock, it was 9:16 PM. She was shocked she slept that long. She wasn't hungry though, not by a long shot. She wasn't even sure anything could enter her mouth. In fact, she didn't want to try to check. There was no point to it, life was a pale white room to her now. A pale, blurry white room she couldn't see through, not that she had the energy for it.

Sometimes, she wondered if she could have done it differently. Alerted Jade to the way Hailey acted and kept her friendship. Maybe she wouldn't be feeling so downcast, so downtrodden. Maybe she wouldn't hate herself so much. But then, she did and there was no changing that. She needed to come to terms with the fact that she'd lost her friends and any credibility whatsoever. Most of all, she'd lost herself.

Grace stood in the hallway, looking into her bag. She walked to the kitchen, had a sip of drink while she grabbed the keys on the counter. She walked back to the hallway and tried to pick up the violin case. She placed it back where it belonged. She stood still for a few seconds, not knowing what to do or where to go from there. She realized that she needed some sort of help. She sighed in defeat.

She went out the door without her bag or case. She didn't look back even once.

***

Victoria, a tall and slim middle aged woman wearing a skirt suit, played with the olive stick in her martini at the bar. She was positively bored just sitting there. She was about to leave when she spotted Grace, sitting by herself. She was checking out Grace, who drained the last drop of her red wine. She saw her chance and took it with two hands.

Victoria said loudly;

"Next one on me." She was bold, even by other people's standards. She pressed closer to Grace, welcoming in her gestures, an air of friendship hovering in her smile.

Grace looked at her quizzically, wondering what she was talking about since that was the very first time she'd seen someone like Victoria. Victoria pointed at her drink and the light of recognition entered into Grace's eyes.

"Oh, thank you," Grace said to her softly. That was one of the things she could manage to say, but felt the need to say more, she was nearly drunk after all. "You're gorgeous, by the way. It's a shame I'm probably ten years too young for you." Grace said, taking a good look at the woman. She was beautiful, Grace could see that much. But there was also something else.

"You're pretty hot yourself. And I'm sure I can pay for counseling to get you over your age issues." Victoria said, already deciding to shoot her shot despite what Grace had said. Grace was shocked and more or less impressed with the older woman.

Grace laughed out loud, unable to believe what she had heard. It was refreshing after all the depressing air the fiasco with Jade and Hailey came with. A moment she needed at this time, a fire that burned with the warmth of taking pains away.

"That or a few drinks and the years will literally slip away." Victoria was getting even bolder, although Grace didn't seem in the mood to have anyone talk to her, she was impressed. The older woman knew exactly what to say; Grace thought.

"I think there is no need for counseling or even a drink. Your one-liners will do the job." Grace replied after much thought, flirting right back.

Victoria was glad she was getting Grace's attention, the smile morphing on her face was one indication of that.

"Well! What are you waiting for then? Set the date lady; come visit me in my apartment." She preferred to be direct, knowing that most women loved other assertive women who knew what they wanted right from the get-go, and hoped Grace was one such woman.

"I'll take you out for a drink. You need to step out of your comfort zone and come to mine." Grace replied, leveling the playing field. Victoria was taken aback, but she had to smile at the guts which Grace showed. She liked it, she liked it a lot. Even more than she expected to.

"Deal." Victoria said, glad that Grace didn't turn her away. She found Grace a good conversationalist, one who could also hold her liquor. She liked that about her, although she more or less liked everything she saw about Grace. But really, what was there not to like? Grace was smart and savvy and funny. The weird thing would have been not liking her.

Grace moved closer to Victoria and grabbed a seat. She knew what Victoria wanted and frankly, she knew that she was down for it. Grace placed her hand gently on Victoria's knee, not needing to say the words to signify her interest. Victoria placed her hand on Grace's back, glad that it worked out just the way she envisioned. She turned to a bartender to order a drink. For both of them. And the secrets of the night.

***

Grace woke up, groggy from sleep. She placed her hand

on her forehead as she tried to get her bearings. The place she was in looked unfamiliar to her. She opened her eyes slightly in order to see better. There was a large portrait of Victoria in front of her, on the wall. She was starting to remember what transpired the night before and the thought sent heat rushing to her cheeks. Victoria walked into the room at that moment, not sparing the time to look at Grace.

"Morning. I'm going to work. Do you want me to give you a ride?" Victoria asked, while not staring at Grace. Grace found it funny, and maybe a little bit childish. They weren't teenagers in heat. They weren't teenagers doing it for the thrill.

"No, thanks. I have a car." Grace replied, not wanting to prolong it any longer than it was necessary. Even though she didn't come with her car to Victoria's place, she didn't want to be in Victoria's mercy any longer than absolutely necessary.

Victoria shrugged, nonchalance coming off her in waves. Although it wasn't unexpected, it stung a little. But Grace shook it off, realizing that they both chose to do what they did. No questions asked.

"You didn't come here by car last night." Victoria said, not bothering to ask again. She still hadn't looked Grace full on the face. She left the bedroom, as though she wanted to be anywhere else but there. Grace just shrugged as she stood up naked, looking for her clothes. It was more of an ordeal since clothes were strewn everywhere but thankfully, she found them. She didn't bother to bathe, wearing her clothes in record time as she put her hair behind her. Finding her pair of shoes was another dilemma that she encountered. After searching the room, she found them behind a box. She exhaled a grateful sigh as she picked them up. She struggled to balance herself to put on her shoes and after a few seconds of trying, she succeeded. She didn't waste any single time as she walked out of the apartment, not looking back even once.

Victoria was having a sip of her coffee when she breezed past the dining and out the door. Victoria heaved a sigh of relief, knowing that she didn't want any commitment with anyone and Grace more or less seemed to have understood it.

"Bye!" Victoria called out to Grace who was already out of earshot. She took a sip of her coffee again. Life was good.

Grace felt a retching in her stomach, an ache in her heart, her eyes burned, so did her throat, and her whole body. She was thoughtless while walking around, unable to believe that she was discarded like a piece of used rag. Even a used rag had more dignity. She wasn't the type of person to jump at other people so she chalked it up to riding the waves of her emotions even though she knew it wasn't true. She genuinely wanted things to be different. Maybe that was her folly. She wiped her nose on the sleeve of her blouse, and kept walking, not daring to look back. She didn't want to, she didn't have any business doing that. Not one single thing. The pain was unbearable, but this she wouldn't do. The bar was low, and she didn't want to take it even lower.

Victoria had shown her how messed up the world could be and even with the years of experience under her belt, she was still shocked at the way she was dismissed and treated no better than an inconvenience to pass the time. It bruised her nerves, in more ways than one.

"I am a full grown woman!" she screamed in her mind.

But, she decided she did all of that to herself and decided that from henceforth, she was going to take her life into her hands and not let anybody treat her like a toy to be played with. Be it Hailey, Jade or Victoria, she wouldn't let anybody come close enough for a repeat episode. That was her resolution, her decision to fully live a detached life.

Grace shaved her head with a pair of clippers. She didn't blink an eye as she watched her beautiful hair reduce in size. Her hair kept dropping on the bathroom floor. It was a statement, one that she had to make. To find herself, to find Grace who had self-respect and couldn't be treated like an afterthought. She wanted to be that person again, not the girl who kept playing at being a woman who knew it all and making mistakes too big to fix. She wasn't that person anymore, she didn't have to be.

She walked toward the shower in slow practiced steps, preparing for the next stage of her rebirth. The next stage of getting her life back. With each step, she got closer and closer. She didn't stop, she didn't falter. She turned the hot water tap on and let the scalding heat sear her skin. She took a hot shower. Her eyes were closed to the world as the heat emanating from the shower peppered her eyelids. Her skin was getting redder and redder. She touched her scalp and washed it. It was painful, more painful than she realized because her scalp was soft to the touch. She didn't wince, didn't so much as betray the pain she was putting her body through. It was being reborn in fire.

The bathroom got even steamier as she bathed, letting the water run down her skin in torrents and rivulets. She was feeling it, the moment she changed. It was an electrifying feeling, her rather painful transition.

Grace wrapped herself in a towel after the hot bath; her mobile on the bedside table was ringing. She checked her phone and saw the caller ID. Jade was calling. She didn't even bother to feel incensed about it, it had been washed away in the shower.

***

Grace was walking to the bus stop with her violin case in her hand. She wore a loose, soft white blouse with soft brown pants. She had big brown sunglasses on, which suited her with her new bald look.

A woman, 40, driving a modern coupe car, keeps looking at Grace. She smiled and held her gaze. Grace smiled back, feeling a sense of tranquility. Her teeth were beautifully white between her red lips. She got on the bus number 102.

A smile was probably the least Grace could have given that, it was what she could afford to give back. After all, she wasn't a cold person that acted all bottled up with people, she didn't intend to be one. But as the bus moved seamlessly to her destination, to everyone's destination, a question kept resonating in her mind, bouncing off every cell in her brain. And, no matter how hard she tried to put it aside, to keep it from touching her mind with its chilling hands, it kept coming back, like a fly that had seen a sweet fruit to follow; "Who was that lady, and why was she smiling at me?" were the questions she asked herself, listening to her breaths.

She was lost in thoughts again, like every other day she took the bus, her mind mulling over issues that existed and bored her down, and issues imagined but had a way to muddle her emotions in the most unpleasant way. Her eyes still on the passing windows on shops, cars and buses, people going about their lives, which Grace thought would be better than hers, the thought of Victoria found its way in her mind, and her heart exploded. She shook her head at the thought, almost breathing stiffly. She reached out for her headphone hung round her neck and she pressed the soft pad of the speaker to her ears, attempting now to maintain her breathing. Grace swallowed and leaned back with a sigh, eyes shut.

Grace hadn't noticed the bus had gotten to her destination as she still had her eyes closed, listening to a jazz song, but only realized it when she felt the bus come to a halt. She got to her feet, and walked swiftly to the exit, trailing behind someone else.

"That was a close one," she said to herself.

Chapter Nine

During their practice in the studio, Tom had managed not to screw this particular one up, and the whole room was delighted to know that. Besides, Tom was good at his game, he knew the right keys to push on his piano, but oftentimes would make his group think he was losing it. Not that they got angry at him, or chided him for it, he was a lovable type of a man, and one couldn't stay crossed at him for long.

"Woah, guys… I guess that would be all for today," said a guy with blond hair with a tint of black shade to it. He was usually the hyper one of the group, pelting everyone to do their best, while he did this with the drum he would always beat with high spirits. Such a person with such demeanor would have gotten to Grace, but she had preferences.

Grace was sitting on a couch in a corner of the studio when Tom walked up to her, taking a seat by her side. He had noticed a change in her, and wanted to know how she was doing, an extension of his good will toward the woman he liked. Such a thing felt like an unavoidable duty to him, he couldn't fight it. He would try, not because Grace didn't like him, but she had been able to leave an impression on him, without her trying or even being conscious about it all. With every look Tom gave Grace, he felt she was slowly becoming a part of him. He didn't mind Grace loving another.

"Are you okay?" he asked her softly.

Grace turned toward him, catching the piercing looks of his coffee-brown eyes, she acted normal toward him, her eyes narrowing and her face sinking in a smile, concealing her emotions the best way she knew how, "I am alright," she said before turning to her phone again.

Tom sinks into the couch, a tide of doubt enveloping him as he thinks of what next he could possibly say to her to open up. He knew she wasn't one to open up that much, except to the night they sat together.

"You don't look alright, you're bald now." Tom pressed on as he always did.

She turned swiftly on the couch, her befuddled eyes sprawled all over Tom's face, "Does being bald mean that something is wrong with me?" she asked sharply, almost drawing the attention of others. Some looked toward them, but quickly turned.

Tom turned toward the others in the far left corner of the room, he wondered what they could be talking about that would have them cackling and laughing, drowning his and Grace's conversation. He turned to Grace again, his eyes searching her face for any hint of discomfort in her but he felt Grace hid whatever she was hiding quite well. That was something he gave her credits for. There was an awkward silence between them, making it seem as though they were meters apart from one another, even though they sat a few inches close.

"That's not what I meant, Grace," he said to her calmly.

"Then, I wondered what you meant by it." she told him, keeping up her act quite expertly, "You know what, Tom? I dont...I don't want to have this conversation, can we change the subject...please?"

There was no need torturing Tom for what he knew nothing about, he was innocent. And making him feel his help wasn't appreciated, would be pushing away the one person who probably cared well enough for her. She has already lost so much, and Tom wouldn't be such a person.

"Sure, we can–"

"Hey, guys? Hope we ain't intruding in the wrong moment, are we?" a bright-faced guy said, he had a necklace round his neck, one made of fiber, and the circle object at the end of it was made of wood. He was a simple fellow, just like the others in the group. And like Sara, Grace liked how chummy he could be with everyone.

"No, Danny, you are not," Tom answered for the both of them, his gaze on Grace who had her gaze on Danny with a cool face.

"Alright, guys, guess what I am about to tell you?" Danny bursted out with a grin, his skin folding at the corners of his eyes, making his face turn pink.

"We will finally be cleaning up after ourselves from now on?" Grace teased, sinking into her with a wry smile.

Danny froze, he knew she had a point, "Nope, that's not it."

"Then, what is it then?" Tom inquired.

Grace was already growing tired of the whole moment, and felt she needed to be somewhere. Not home, but somewhere else she could go and refresh her head, it was heating up in ways she couldn't understand and it bothered her greatly. Danny's smile, or Sara's innocent eyes couldn't help.

"We have a gig, guys! A show!" Danny's words were so sudden, and his voice so high, it could have passed through the door and someone else would hear him. Perhaps, share in his joy.

The others started clapping, they all had grins spread out on their faces, eyes narrowed and spirits high all over the room. It was something they had been wanting to do for a while now, a moment they had been waiting for. A gig! Finally a gig. It must have felt exquisite in their minds, the feeling of having to play good music to the hearing of an audience. And as they clapped and smiled with an electrifying cheer, their minds were already picturing that day.

"Wow, t-t-that's great news… We definitely need to celebrate this," Tom said in high spirits.

With a glee in her soft voice, hands clasped against her breasts, "That was exactly what I had suggested, but the guys said it was a small gig and so, the need isn't there," Sara's voice suddenly took a pitiable undertone, as though trying to draw some support from Tom and Grace.

"That's because it isn't, actually," said Danny quickly.

"But you sounded as though it was worth celebrating, you just did it here a while ago," Tom told him, making Danny rethink his words.

"Yeah, but then—"

"But then, we were thinking of keeping the energy till a bigger gig comes up," a baritone voice cut through Danny's words.

"Yeah, something bigger than this one. We are to only perform at a local club for some guests at the club," Said another man who looked older than the rest, and had a protruding belly, a boozer he was.

"How many times have we gotten gigs before, Adam? Tell me, I will be delighted to know," Tom asked him, pelting the question at him, leaving him lost for a bit for a bit.

Sara was delighted she had someone who saw things as she did, feeling up the hole that had been created by the others. As the others laughed at her reason for having a small drink over their big moment, she felt alone as they told her the gig wasn't big enough. Their cackling made things worse for Sara's mood too, but with Tom, it made a difference, and she finally had a sense that she wasn't alone. But, there were three who weren't in support of celebration, Tom was the only one supporting her, leaving one other person to finally decide. Grace.

She had been quiet all through the back and forth her friends were having, lost in her thoughts. She did that quite often when she felt her energy shouldn't be spent toward a particular thing, or when she needed to be away in the midst of a crowd. Away in her head. She only watched the argument and counterargument going on between them, she was exhausted and she didn't quite know why. But, she felt she ought to be in another place.

"Well, Grace? Where do you belong?" Sara asked her. She knows Grace was the only person that hasn't been saying much lately, and although it bothered her, she felt it wasn't the time or place to ask her.

Grace gave a quick look at her, Sara's deep brown eyes fixed on her puzzled face, "Errm… well, I think we should celebrate, this is indeed a big one for us."

Grace felt content with her reply. It was the best she could come up with, but it came out better than she had thought, and she hoped her colleagues got it. And they did as Tom howled into the air in a convincing yell, bringing to Danny the ridiculousness of his idea, he looked at the other two as well and made them feel they had been wrong not to have a drink over such a moment. Tom swam in the deepening feeling the other three were having, laughing and poking them in a teasing way.

Sara, however, only smiled. She didn't howl like Tom, or shriek like she used to when she was overjoyed. She only smiled, a close-lipped smile, and Grace could see Sara had her doubts about her response. She hoped Sara won't come gauding her answers.

As she had hope, Sara never came for answers. She laughed and smiled and cheered with the others at the bar, as though nothing else mattered. She could see the whiteness of her teeth, the size of the two front teeth, she thought Sara's teeth made her smile look good, her face brighter, the two front teeth hadn't been too big and it made her face simple and neat. No much noise. She also knew someone with such a bright smile, hers was enthralling and Grace loved every bit of it.

The group's celebration over their gig lasted less than an hour, and while they left, Grace had told them she would like to stay back a little while longer. She wasn't ready to leave yet, she told them. Others laughed and teased her, Tom and Sara only saw a shadow of her, a shadow of the Grace they had once known. Sara had felt compelled to speak with Grace, but had decided to leave for another day, her boss called.

As Grace sat in the bar, a gleaming bottle of whiskey sat on her right and a cup before her waiting to be filled the fourth time in the 11 minutes she had been there, she thought of the possible things she could do if she was at home, and when nothing came, she kept pouring in more whiskey for herself.

And then, she felt a tap on her shoulder. Her head was resting on the table as she had drank herself to a halt, unable to do much, but lay her head on the folded cushion that was her hands. She felt the tap again, followed by a voice. She thought it was Hailey's, and her eyes bolted open, with a shiver running down her spine. Grace looked up, and her face fell.

"Hello, I'm Olivia." said a familiar face Grace had seen before.

Chapter Ten

She was beaming with a smile, the woman. Her perfectly white teeth still maintained their white under the yellow of the bar they were in. She was a lean figure, tall and graceful in the way she walked, she could easily be mistaken for a model. Her face was oval-shaped and her eyes a pale grey, her skin looked amazing to Grace as she felt the need to ask her about it. But, she wasn't feeling the moment. Grace didn't really like her dress, a white and black skin-hug dress, with a small belt round her small waist. Grace watched her from head to toe, and got a glimpse of her footwear, her heels perhaps, black and simple, and Grace immediately knew Olivia must be a simple lady.

"I'm sorry, I couldn't help myself when I saw you here in the bar. Which is why I decided to come up here." Olivia said, pushing her dark hair out of her face.

Grace stayed quiet for a moment, thinking of what she could say to her, knowing she wasn't in the mood to entertain anybody, letting Olivia know would save her a lot of trouble. For Olivia actually.

"And now you're here, what can I help you with?" Grace dragged her words, almost letting out a hiccup as she drew in a breath. Her face drooped, and she looked sleepy.

"I saw you earlier, and I absolutely love your style." Olivia said to her, taking a seat quickly in front of Grace, who didn't like where this was going.

Grace made a drowsy face, as though she would face asleep any moment the following minute. Olivia watched her with absolute interest, wide-eyed and with a grin rippling through her face.

"And what exactly did you like about my style, huh?" Grace asked.

"Well, I think you're strong, forward with your actions, and just…beautiful at it," Olivia said, striking a nerve in Grace.

"Really?" Grace wasn't impressed, her voice a mocking tone and she felt a bit of a bile taste in her mouth. It could have been the alcohol, but Olivia's gestures only irritated Grace more.

"Yes. Really. You look like a representation of what modern women should be like; strong and bold with their actions when it suits them, not minding what the repercussions would be." She sounded convincing, but Grace wasn't looking like it.

"What about getting drunk in a bar? Is that strong enough for you? Your definition of a strong woman?" Grace asked her to pull the rug under her carpet, but Olivia only smiled, her face becoming brighter with every minute spent with Grace.

"I do not think you come here everyday to booze yourself, I had seen you earlier with your friends when you all came to drink. All of them drank, they all laughed, including you, but yours felt as though you were forcing it, trying to maintain what you wanted your friends to see, and not the other part of you," she said to Grace, who held her gaze with Olivia's eyes.

Grace stared for a moment, as though trying to collect her thoughts together, to piece before she could utter, and a moment later, she shook her head and made to leave the bar.

Grace started packing up her things and her violin case, "You know what? I am out of here. I cannot sit here and talk about being strong, only to be given the news of a century."

"What news?"

"You won't get it. No one does."

Olivia didn't press forward as she watched Grace walk out the door, swayed right, and then left, holding on to chairs and tables in the bar, so as not to fall to the floor. Olivia said nothing, she felt she didn't need to as it may only, probably, aggravate Grace, and she wasn't ready for any emotional outburst. Grace thought she had had one too many whiskeys. As Grace left, Olivia shrugged off the moment, and poured in some whiskey Grace had left for herself. She hoped they would meet again, but that wasn't quite the same for Grace.

As Grace sat in her tub, immersed in the warmth of the water she was in, she felt as though she was carrying much more than she could handle. Her body gave off the signs she wasn't herself, she had said to herself she would act differently. But every time she walked, she walked with anxiety and uncertainty in every part of her being, trying to keep her head above water.

Grace was still holding on, her thoughts about Hailey, she still recounted the moments they had shared together, it felt surreal to her that one person could feel so much love for another, give out so much and risk so much, so the person you love would feel safe and happy with you. It felt surreal, her moments with Hailey, as seconds passed, minutes, hours, even days, an emptiness in her kept spreading its tentacles all over her, gripping her ever tightly. She hated it, and wished it would all go away.

She stared into a distance she didn't realize when a stream of tears had rolled down her eyes, the bitter taste coming back again, the churning in her stomach, the burn in her heart. It was all back. Grace realized, and quickly wiped her tears, she reached out for a bottle on tub, and gulped on its content with ferocity, with hunger, and grimaced a shrunken face as she put down the bottle. She sighed, her eyes closed and her chest heaving, such a moment she had always dreaded, and now it is staring in the face as they shared a tub together. Grace sighed again, her face drooping, she sunk into the warm water she was in. And slowly, she was totally submerged as water rippled above.

***

It was a fine day, the sun was out and it felt comforting to the body, people went about their daily lives selling and interacting with one another, and it seemed there couldn't be a mistake written in today's atmosphere. Grace, for one, loved it. The beams from the yellow sun, she felt like staying under its rays forever, the smell of food coming from a nearby restaurant or diner, or folks with strong, but pleasant colognes. It was certainly a day to be free, to have a breath of fresh air, and feel light in your own skin. It was a day Grace had made a mental note to put everything behind her. To let it go. Everything.

"It is not worth it." Grace had said in the bathtub, her head beneath the water.

Grace was on her way to a grocery store, her skin a tint of yellow as the sun had turned it yellowish-brown. She was also wearing a white T-shirt, and a walnut brown pants, and walked with an air of near aloofness until her eyes caught something – someone – and she stood for a moment to watch.

It was a couple, or perhaps not, Grace didn't know. Girls hugged themselves in ways one wouldn't know if they had something going between them. The tight hugs, breasts bumping each other, the giggling and cheerful smiles, the kissing. Perhaps, one could know when two girls didn't have something between them. The way they kissed, or the playfulness of it. The two girls Grace watched, however, didn't kiss in a manner that was deemed *'playful.'* They didn't, and it struck Grace in her bones that she felt it quiver.

One of them had walked up to the other, somewhat walking and running, she was trotting, hands open for the other to lock in, her tortilla brown hair lifting into the air, her orange face beaming with a smile. The sun must have made her face so. The other had darker hair, it was a bit shorter than the other, and she was a bit fleshier too, more curvy. The orange-faced lady was much more slender, but the two women were simply beautiful, and Grace thought these were women who had much more to give to one another.

She stayed a little longer watching them, the way the two women kissed, the way they held their hands locked together, the wrinkle of their eyes, the glint of love and care in their pale-colored eyes. Grace couldn't see their eyes, but that didn't matter. They were talking now, and she imagined what they could be talking about. She imagined they would go to a coffee shop perhaps, and have a cup of coffee, to catch up on many things. They looked as though they hadn't seen each other in a while, the way they hugged and their smiles suggested so, but Grace shrugged that away as well. It didn't matter.

Grace's eyes followed them as they started walking away, hands still laced together and each smile and giggle from them made her swallow. It made her heart sink unto itself, and her stomach shriveled into ugly lines of muscle, something that couldn't be looked at. She suddenly felt nauseated, something coming up her throat, and she continued her walk to the grocery, maintaining her gaze away from the couple. She had finally concluded they were one.

She was at an aisle where dairy products were sold, carefully running her eyes from one milk bottle to the other, a yogurt pack to the other, taking the ones she needed. The thoughts about the couple earlier had fizzled out of her mind quicker than she had expected, it gladdened her, her head would no longer tingled with thoughts that would leave her in a slithering line of ups and downs. She hated mood swings, although she managed it well much more than others.

She left the aisle and into a section that had fruits and

veggies, she loved fruits, or anything that isn't an apple. She hated apples, and wouldn't drink anything that had it. Unless, it didn't taste like apple. Grace had always had a sophisticated state of mind, that most things she did were mostly subconscious.

Grace walked through the aisle in a distant state, aloof to most things around her, or the people around her. She didn't seem to see them most of the time, her eyes were on the apples and bananas and berries that sat clean in their corners where they were placed. Then, a song came on in the store, and a while later, Grace raised her head to it. She was suddenly warm, and her heart started beating faster than normal, her breath slowing down. Nostalgia was wrapping its hands around her, inside her, even her heart, and a longing filled every breath she took.

Grace's head jerked up swiftly, a familiar voice was coming her way, but she wasn't sure who it was. And so, she stood still, her eyes turned to her right, her heart paced with every minute that passed, and her mind coming up with different possibilities.

"It could be anybody," she thought.

She shouldn't be here, she ought to continue her walk, but here she was, still as a log, listening to her breaths as her chest pushed and sank. The voice got closer, Grace could hear it, the softness, the flow to it, the small throaty ring to it. It was certainly a voice she had heard. And it was about to come out from the other corner. Grace averted her eyes quickly.

She heard it coming toward her, this voice, and she felt an urge to look. And so, she did. She looked up to what might appear to be Hailey and Jade, her heart in her stomach, but was relieved when she saw a man and woman who strikingly have the same voice Hailey and Jade had, and had blamed it all on her imagination.

"I think I may be losing my mind." Grace said to herself.

She picked the fruits she needed, and dashed quickly toward the corner the man and woman had come through, and she froze on entering the next aisle. She froze, as familiar eyes stared right back at her, with the same consternation Grace had on her eyes.

"Hey," Grace said to Jade, her throat constricting as the word flowed out of her lips, riddled with anxiety.

"Hey." Jade responded back, not knowing what she would do with such a moment. None of them did. The air of gripping anxiety blacked out their thoughts about anything, Grace was speechless the most.

Jade looked toward Hailey, who had her eyes on a shelf with all kinds of biscuits on it, not looking at Grace. Grace wasn't looking at Hailey as well, she felt no need to do so. Hailey wasn't deserving of her gaze, she didn't deserve to be looked at, after the betrayal, after leaving her to her own feelings to soak up what was left, the bitterness, the broken pieces. Hailey's stay with her would have made a difference even as Jade found out. They would have still been together, a couple living a life of fulfillment, in their arms, their breaths teasing their naked skins, but Hailey left too, giving her nothing to hold on to.

A relationship worth saving was the one she had with Jade. Grace felt Hailey must have known that by now, she only had her eyes on Jade, the friend she didn't want to betray.

Jade took Hailey's hand, "Come on, let's go."

Hailey looked up, and her eyes crashed with Grace's, her legs turned to water, she felt too weak to stand, and she could swear Jade could hear her heart. Grace turned her eyes from Hailey to Jade.

"Jade, wait. Please, don't do this." Grace said, standing in Jade's way.

Jade scoffed, her eyes narrowed as a sneer formed on her lips, "Watch me, Grace," she said stiffly, walking round her.

Grace stepped in her way again, "Please, Jade, let's talk, you are making a mistake" she said to her. Grace only wanted to make their relationship work, to restore it to how it was, the laughs, the cheers, the jeering at each other's fancies, and the feeling that you have somewhere there, someone who's ready to have you in their arms when you are falling. She wanted Jade back as that someone.

"I tried to forget you," Jade suddenly said. She had been looking at Grace for a while now, knowing she wouldn't step out of the wall. Grace was bigger and fleshier, she stood no chance. Hailey couldn't do much either, she only stood there, sinking to the floor, though she stood tall in their midst.

"I know, and I couldn't forgive myself for what I did. Please, can we start over?" Grace asked, she could herself as she was about to cry. It was croaky and brittle, and she hated it when such a thing was happening to her. A penance she must go through if Jade is to accept her back, she thought.

Jade made to say something, her finger pointing at Grace under the white florescent lights of the store, but she held back, she couldn't say it. She didn't want to, there was no need for it. Her gaze was still fixed on Grace, her mouth heavy with words, words she couldn't let go.

Jade made to go again, clutching a mute Jade by the hand. Grace didn't step in her way this time, she allowed her to go, she needed to. She could see the reluctance in her eyes, she knew Jade couldn't be gauded to have a cup of coffee with her, to sit and talk about old times, old mistakes, to share a laugh again. So, she let her go, watching as Hailey walked beside her hopelessly, a dark, cold air overwhelming her. She knew Hailey felt she wasn't in the movie they were acting, for the only cast was she and Jade.

But as they walked on, their heels giving off a *click-clack* against the store's floors, Hailey looked back, and for the first time in a long while, Grace saw in her eyes the same longing she had seen the first time they shared a gaze.

Chapter Eleven

Grace got home feeling more drained than she had ever felt. Her face drooped again, her eyes sunken and tired, she walked over to the kitchen and dropped the items she had bought from the grocery store on the kitchen counter. She went over to the fridge and wrapped her hand around a bottle of wine, and with a forlorn expression, she trudged to the living area and sunk herself into a couch, the bottle already in her mouth, gulping up the wine.

She turned on the television, hoping it would help get her mind off what she was feeling. The television tuned to a news channel and Grace changed it quickly. She had no interest in the state of affairs of the country, she had a lot to deal with herself. She tuned it to a station she knew wouldn't make her listen to her emotion, to wash over her like a running stream, and have her brood over an uncertain moment she knows won't come back. A channel that talked about animals was her best bet. Animals can evoke fond memories, or have one tangle in the net of their emotions.

But, it didn't help the station, it didn't take away the series of hurt in her heart, or stop her breath from burning. It did none of that, and she hated it. She hated her mind still drifted to Jade and Hailey and their encounter from earlier. She stopped watching the television and she laid down on the couch, her head pricking against the couch as she had started growing new hairs, she was facing the ceiling now, her eyes on the whiteness of it. She suddenly thought what a white paint smelt like, or felt like on the skin.

She thought of other things that could keep her from thinking of Hailey's eyes, the emotions in them, she knew those emotions, but doesn't want anything to do with it. Yet, her heart kept pricking with every thought of it, skipping beats when she thought of her smiles, when she smiled. Hailey. In a way, Grace wasn't totally honest with herself, and she knew it.

Grace's attention was soon drawn to a knock on the door, and Hailey swept through her mind. Though, she knew it wouldn't be Hailey. The knock on the door came again, and Grace had no other choice but to go check who it was.

She walked up to the door, her legs dragging against the floor, she heard a voice come through the door. It was Sara.

Sara ran her eyes all over Grace, awashed with concern, "You look like a wreck right now."

"Hey, Sara, come on inside," she said walking to the living room. Sara followed closely.

"What happened? You don't look so good " Sara inquired, facing her on the same couch Grace sat on.

"It's nothing you should worry yourself about. Just having one of those low days in my life, it's nothing serious," she said, trying to shift Sara's attention from her. Grace was able to appear as normal as she could, to brighten up her face with a smile, her brows raised up. She tried to make

Sara perceive as little as possible what was underneath the wreck that is her eyes, but Sara kept staring into those eyes, her brown eyes mirroring Sara. Grace tried to hold onto her gaze, to seem as if the roof was still up, at least till Sara was convinced.

"Well, if you say so," Sara said, shrugging the matter aside. Grace swallowed in relief, her muscles relaxing as Sara is smiling again. A smile she likes to see.

"So, what brings you here this afternoon? Have you got something for me?" Grace asked. The room seemed too tense for her, for Grace, and she wanted to clear it up, to raise it high above their heads, and let a free type of air in. The type that won't choke them all.

"Well now, you make it seem as though I cannot I can't visit my friend anymore, is that what you are saying?" Sara said, teasing Grace into a state she was glad to have found herself. Her mind was loosening now.

Grace gasped, "Where are my manners, my apologies, Sara. Let me get you something, I've got wine, you want some?" Grace brandished the bottle of wine at her.

"I think that would be nice, thank you."

"Alright then, let me go get a cup for you. I will be right back."

Grace entered the room a few minutes later with two glass cups in her, one for her, and the other for Sara. Before Sara's arrival, she had been drinking right from the bottle. She smiled as she poured in the liquor for the both of them, trying to bring up a conversation, the air was already awkward to them, making it worse may deepen it. Grace wasn't ready for that.

Grace walked toward Sara and handed her a glass, taking a seat, "How's work so far? You know, at the office?" Grace asked.

"Work's fine, Grace. It can be daunting sometimes, but I tell you we are surfing the waves as it comes, you get me?"

"I would be lying if I say I don't," Grace said cackling, "Because I totally do," she said laughing a hearty laughter.

"Yeah... that reminds me," Sara said, her face flushed, "I came to tell you our gig is in two days...so get ready, you hear me." she said with a high-pitched voice, swirling her arms as she spoke.

"That's terrific news... Okay, okay, okay, who's taking us there?" Grace asked as she jumped on the couch, her body suddenly jittery from the news. It was as though she was being tickled in her underarms, she beamed ceaselessly, so did Sara.

"Danny. He would be taking us there with his van. And yes, he has a van."

"Woah, I didn't know he had a van."

"He does now, bought it yesterday. He was going to surprise you all at our next meeting tomorrow, but I guess it won't come as a surprise to you since you are aware now."

"Don't worry, I can pretend. He won't even know I have known about his van."

"Yeah."

Silence. But, it was a good kind of silence. The type they can bask in, the type they can allow their imagination run wild, to hold them in the euphoria of being able to perform before an adoring audience. Grace and Sara, gripped by the feeling, they could see themselves, the audience looking at them, cheering as they finish performing, receiving an applause from them. A flushed feeling rushed through them both, but Grace had something to say.

"When are you going to tell me you and Danny are together?" she said with a smile, gazing at Sara, who had just choked on her drink, with a piercing look on her face. "I am pretty sure you thought I didn't know, right?"

"How did you know?..." Sara asked bemused at how Grace found out about her ruse. It dawned on her she couldn't hide it from everyone, not Grace.

"Of course, I will know. You think I don't see how you two look at each other? Please, you may have had others fooled, but not your girl, Grace," she said, basking in her own astuteness.

"Well… that was another surprise we wanted to unveil to you guys," she said, "No, not tomorrow as with his van. We wanted to tell you all when we felt it was time," Sara added the moment she sensed Grace wanted to say something.

Grace sank into her seat, a comforting smile on her face, "But, why did you choose to keep it away from us? Aren't we all friends after all or just a band?"

"We are! It's just that, we wanted it to be quiet for a while, no one had to know about us. We wanted it to be just the two of us, in our own little world. And when we feel it is time for us to come out and say it, to show others what we are, even when someone might not approve, we will surely come out and say it. That was our plan."

"Hmm, even when someone might not approve, you say?"

"Yes. I had a boyfriend, he's clingy, but I liked him. When I fell out of love with him, I had to keep my relationship with Danny a secret, till it was time to tell him I was leaving. He felt hurt, I was hurt, but it was probably for the best."

Grace listened to Sara, her mind pacing from one thought to the other, more times than she could realize, and she tried to weigh what Sara had just told her. She was silent, more silent than she could ever be, but she saw Sara didn't mind, she was sipping on her drink and knew that she was trying to understand the whole thing. Sara gave her time, Grace thought, and appreciated her for that. She knew when words were needed and when silence fits the moment.

"You are right, Sara," Grace said, Sara's attention reverting back to her, almost spilling the wine she had just poured for herself, "It was probably for the best."

***

Later that day, in the evening as the sun had gone down and the moon almost in full view, Grace sat in her tub, letting her mind take her away, as it always does. She thought of Sara, and thought what she and Danny did was laughable, keeping her relationship from the rest of the group.

She laughed a little as she soaked in the tub, picturing Sara and Danny as they stared at one another. Sara's warm, carefree smiles beaming at Danny, with an air of affection meant only for him. She pictured them at other places, and she laughed as she did so. The whole thing seemed ridiculous to her, she had known them for a while now, and expected anyone would date another in the room, then it struck her. Tom was after her as well, but she reassured herself that he must have got on already. Yes, he must have.

Such a line of thought made her remember Hailey, and this time, she didn't fight, or put up her defenses. She allowed the thought of her to fill her mind, like a cloud or gas spreading itself all over her mind, her body. She leaned back, and closed her eyes, letting Hailey walk in.

The sky was very cloudy that day. Thick, puffy clouds floated lazily past in the sky, above the city down below, the houses, the shops, the cars, and the office buildings. And most especially, a coffee shop.

Grace had driven to Hailey's coffee shop. She knew Hailey would be around on that day, and had gone to have a word with her. It was a Thursday, there was no mistaking it. Their last meeting might have been a disaster, but she was ready to make Hailey know her feelings toward her. She might have left without knowing how she felt toward her, not giving her a chance, so Grace thought of creating one.

Grace to the coffee shop, she sat in her car for a moment, wondering if she was doing the right thing. She couldn't possibly be doing the right thing.

"What if Jade was there with her? What would I say? How will I handle it? How will I look at Jade?" she thought within her. But then, she made the decision to get out of her car, and walk into Hailey's coffee shop, damning the consequences.

So, she got out, and walked through the door, the bell above her rang, giving away her presence. But, Hailey didn't notice, her back was turned to Grace. She was serving a customer, a man in his late thirties or so, big with rough-looking skin, and she was relieved that Hailey hadn't seen her yet. Though, it didn't last for long as Hailey's deep eyes met hers the moment she turned. Everything else around them stood still. They stood still as well, with only their eyes doing the talking. There was pleading and regrets in their eyes, it was unblinking, the edges getting glossy with every minute they stood gazing at each other. Hailey's face started to get warm, and Grace knew that feeling, the feeling of having to see someone whom you think you've lost, and will never see again, a form of rekindled love and hope. Grace saw all written all over Hailey's eyes, and she was drawn to it.

Hailey started walking toward Grace, Grace rose her foot toward Hailey as well, and they were soon breasts to breast, their warm, pleading eyes sinking into the other, and at that moment, nothing else mattered. At least, to Hailey. Her heart leaped in ecstasy on seeing Grace again, her stomach tingled for her touch again, and her skin came alive, bringing back the same feeling she had felt when she and Grace had shared a deep gaze. To Hailey, nothing else mattered.

But, Grace couldn't see it that way as she turned swiftly and left the coffee shop, unable to hold Hailey's welcoming gaze. Hailey stood there, shocked to a stop, her face changing to one of despair and shattered hope, confusion sinking deeper and deeper inside of her as she saw Grace drive onto the road, her car moving away till she had disappeared into a corner. Her mind couldn't make out what had just happened.

Grace couldn't do it. She couldn't bring herself to tell Hailey how she felt, the nights she had stayed up thinking of their moment, her heart beating for the time they would finally have stared into each other's eyes again, or stay up playing the violin together again like that dream of hers. Maybe, they would be naked again. Maybe, Grace would be the one doing the playing. Grace had a lot to say, but she couldn't say it. She drove back to her place, her lips quaking in angst, her eyes misty with burning tears, she couldn't see well and had to dab at her eyes regularly. She hated her decision, coming out to the coffee shop, only to drive back home.

Grace could also remember her time with Jade, when she and Jade still did things together. It was before she had met Hailey, before Jade had met Hailey. She thought her life was so much peaceful then, though she doesn't regret knowing Hailey, she was a person she wouldn't throw out in the trash during a cold night, Hailey grew on her and she long for the day they might once again hold each other, but then, her life before Hailey, was calm and undisturbed.

She was in her living room when she heard a knock on the door, she was watching her favorite and was reluctant to knock. She thought the person would go away when no one answered. She picked her remote control and turned down the volume, a way to show she wasn't home.

The knocks came in again, followed by a familiar voice, jerking Grace's ears awake to the voice. She saw it was brittle and it cracked, but it belonged to someone she has heard the voice from before. It came again, brittle and cracked, and she knew it instantly, running toward the door. She opened it up and Jade stood there with deep, tired eyes, black round it, and her mascara running a long line down her face due to tears.

Grace stretched her hands in a hug without saying a word and Jade slumped into it, crying, her head on Grace's breasts, smearing her mascara all over her yellow T-shirt. She pulled Jade away from the door, shutting it and made their way to the living room couch.

"What happened?" Grace asked, taking Jade's gaze up to hers. Her voice was filled with care and comfort, and wanted Jade to feel she was

at the right place. In a way, Jade already knew.

Jade sniffed, "another relationship gone bad, that's all." she tried to regain her voice.

Grace most times didn't know how to judge matters such as this, she felt it and knew how it hurt, but didn't know the right words to use. She wanted to say something that would make Jade feel less of a wreck, though she could see Jade was trying to be strong, she knew Jade was deeply hurt.

"It's alright, Jade, this will pass too" These were the best words she thought would make a difference for what she was going through. She looked at Jade, searching her face, hoping it made the effect she was looking for.

"Did you know what she said to me before she left?" Jade said, looking at the television. The show on television meant little to her at that moment, her heart ached so badly she couldn't concentrate, she couldn't think of much. Her pains just hung there in her eyes for everyone to see.

"What did she say?" Grace asked softly. Maybe letting her vent a bit about her pain might help her ease it in the first place, and fighting it, telling her not to say anything about it would mean Jade would have to bottle up all her emotions inside.

Jade swallowed, her eyes on Grace, "She said she doesn't see a future with me, that she doesn't think we were meant for each other. A match, she said. After one year of dating, she comes up with an idiotic excuse of not been a match. How foolish of me to be living in a world where I wasn't accepted. I am so stupid."

Grace froze at those words; "I am so stupid," and she realized she had put Jade in the same place again.

Grace let out a breath of resentment, she got out of the tub, and cleaned herself up. She walked to her room, and sank into her bed, her thoughts still racing about that day, the day she left Hailey without saying a word. Her heart burned anytime the thought came up, and she closed her eyes, her naked body curled up in bed, waiting for sleep to take it all away.

But, it doesn't really go away, that she knew.

Chapter Twelve

The next morning, Grace woke up, her naked skin feeling every fabric of her bedspread, she hadn't realized she slept naked and had thought it odd. She had slept naked before, not that it mattered, but it felt different.

Grace got out of bed, resisting the urge of thinking too much about her sleeping naked, she had known what caused it, and didn't want to bring it back to her memory. She just wanted a peaceful morning, and so, she walked to her fridge, after getting herself ready for the morning, and started making breakfast. She had a jazz song on, something to make her feel better after the thoughts of last night. She cooked and bumped her head to the rhythm, and moved her body to the flow of the song, singing when she knew the part that came up. It was a song by *Julie London,*

Go slow, ooh honey, take it easy on the curves
When love is slow, ooh honey,
What a tonic for my nerves.

A smile soon appeared on her face, her mood was turning to the sun, bright and airy from the song she was listening to, stirring her eggs and vegetables the way she liked it, and getting her coffee ready. But, another thing that made her smile was the thought of Sara and Danny, and the van she was going to see. It was a cause of excitement for her, and she couldn't wait to be there, with them. She could see them all smiling and laughing, and making merry, teasing Danny a little bit as they always do. It was a moment she couldn't wait to see.

An hour later, she was ready, though she still had more than an hour to spare before going over to the studio. Grace thought of going outside for a moment, to have a smoke or two, before it was time to make her way to the studio.

On her way downstairs, she bumped into a familiar face, a face she had seen before, but hadn't given enough audience to. The face beamed at her, and in surprise, Grace beamed back. She had to beam back, she had to make her know she wasn't mean, she had been mean the last time, but this time was different and she couldn't let it be ruined by anything.

The both of them smiled, and Olivia knew Grace might not have been in a good mood the last time they met, and had allowed her go without pressing forward, setting off an already drunk Grace. But, today was a day she was grateful for, seeing Grace in a much lighter tone.

"Hi, remember me?" Olivia asked, her red lips still maintaining her smile.

Grace wore a bewildered face, "Yes, I do, but I can't seem to remember the name."

"Olivia, we met officially at the bar. Although, I will count this moment as the official one as we are actually having a full conversation," Olivia said.

Grace laughed, holding the pale blue eyes that stared into hers, "I am so sorry for last time, I didn't know what came over me."

"It is okay," Olivia said, waving her hands in the air, pushing the issue aside, "You were drunk when we met, so I don't blame you. I blame the whiskey for being so good and doing its work."

Grace laughed again, she thought Olivia to be quite interesting, knew what to say and her red lipstick was striking to her. But, she hadn't known what she was doing here, or who she was looking for, and felt the need to ask without coming off as rude or distrusting.

"You look beautiful, a lot better than last time. I can see that this is the real you," Olivia said, climbing up a few more steps to where Grace was, and she smelled her cologne.

"Yes, I like to keep it simple with my life, and you also look nothing short of being beautiful yourself. You also look amazing, I loved your lipstick by the way." Grace said to her, returning the gesture.

"Oh, I don't get much compliments on my lipstick, thank you. Maybe, when we get to know each other, I will tell you the brand I buy!" Olivia told her.

Grace could see what Olivia was doing, and thought it to be quite bold, striking her unaware. This atmosphere around her, the confidence, the way she held people's gaze, the smile, the gleaming white teeth, the lipstick. She liked it, she liked that someone was this enigmatic and elegant. There was no harm in letting herself swim in the moment, the moment with Olivia, to have someone who she could do and nothing else. Her heart wasn't a rollercoaster of emotions that would be rotating between individuals and anyone that comes into her life. She had said to herself that night that no one would take her for granted anymore, enough hurt had been endured, and now she was only going to ride in the moment.

"Uhhm, you came to see someone?" Grace asked.

"Yes, I did, I came to see a cousin of mine who lives here, but now I am with you, I am second-guessing it."

Grace grimaced, "Okay. I was thinking outside for a smoke, want to join me?"

Olivia made a gesture that Grace should lead the way, "Sure, let's go."

Grace and Olivia talked over some rolls of cigarettes that day, exchanging stories about their time in the city, their careers and love lives. Her time with Olivia was she liked, she laughed, she cackled, she stifled a laughter, and most of all, she saw someone who had had the same experience she had had with love. And, in a way, she didn't feel so alone.

"My goodness! I should be going, I have…this thing that I want to do right now," Grace said as she checked her phone for the time.

"Oh, I can drop you off, where are you going?" Olivia asked, standing up.

"No, Olivia, don't worry. Maybe, next time," she said, going through a door that led to the stairs.

"You forgot to give me your number!" Olivia screamed, but Grace didn't open the door again. She was gone.

***

Grace walked briskly along the streets, trying to make it to bus 102. Her loose, sweeping skirt moved in tandem with air as she walked, slapping against her skin with every step she took. She had thought of using her car as she was late, but thought she could still catch up. She had never driven herself in her car to the studio, she loved taking the bus, but today, it seemed she had made a big mistake. But luckily, she made it to the bus in time, and she hopped in, sinking into a seat in relief, her muscles relaxing, though they burned from her power walking.

A few minutes later, she was at the studio, and she ran up the building, and into the room. She walked in panting slightly, her chest heaving with exhaustion, she masked it, but the stunned eyes that looked back at her were certain she had run all the way here.

"Hey, sorry I'm late. I got up with something, and hadn't noticed time had passed by like that," Grace said, taking a seat to rest her nerve. Her pacing, wrecking nerves and her burning legs.

"Are you okay, Grace?" Tom asked her, sitting beside her.

"I-I'm fine, I just want to rest here a bit." Grace said. She had her head leaned on the couch, her eyes were shut close, and her breaths were heavy with cold air running down her nostrils. She hated to wait for something, but one thing she hated again, was to run after it after she had nearly missed it. The bus was one of those few things.

"Well, guys," Danny said, calling the attention of others, "Since everyone is here, I have got something to show you all."

Grace knew what it was going to be, and wished she could stay where she was a little longer, to sink into the couch and bring her breath to normal. But, she couldn't do that, or afford to do it, she wasn't a bad friend and didn't want to appear as one. Sara already knew Grace knew, and may understand if Grace said she wasn't coming with them, but would the other understand? Grace knew the likely answers to that. Grace wasn't a talker in the group, and they knew her, but how much does she know about their opinions about her? What were their thoughts about her whenever she wasn't around? She had already learnt of the van, but had promised Sara Danny would think everyone was unaware.

"Well, Grace? Aren't you coming?" Tom said to her, beckoning her to get up.

Grace sighed, "Alright, Tom, let's go."

Tom offered his hand in a gesture to help, "Come here, let me help you."

Grace brushed his hands away, refusing his help, "Do not bother, Tom, I can walk,"

Tom left her alone, walking behind her closely. He still cared for her, still wanted Grace to see that he could be enough for her, but all Grace did was push him away, closing her doors of emotions toward him. Tom didn't care, he didn't care that Grace was that way with him, or had feelings for another, for anytime he saw Grace, he saw a woman who needed all the love she could ever get. And he wanted to be the one who gave this love, sadly, it seemed it wasn't meant to be. Tom's spirit, however, hasn't waned due to it, and still had his feelings toward Grace.

They went outside, behind the building, and into an open ground, a basketball court, where the van was parked. And a few moments later, they were near the van, it was covered with a pale grey sheet, and some of them got a hint of what it may be, though they didn't say a thing to ruin the surprise. They only walked in silence, waiting for Danny to do the unveiling, he looked ecstatic about it all. The wide grin on his face, the wrinkle to his eyes, the folding of his cheek. Grace had thought Danny's face would freeze if he didn't ease up on the smile.

"Alright, guys, I want to present to you my…my van," Danny said, his beaming being the brightest among them.

Grace's face beamed as well, and she had been wrong about not getting excited about the Danny van unveiling. She already knew about the van, a knowledge already known shouldn't have much of an effect on the person who knew it, but Grace stood in their midst with a face that can't stop her smiles from ceasing. She watched as Danny took off the sheet, exposing a black, shining van.

Everyone cheered, walking over to Danny to shake his hand. Grace walked over to him and gave him a hug, looking into his eyes deeply. Danny was happy as well, but his joy was elevated when he saw that his friends were happy for him as well.

"Congratulations, Danny, well deserved." Grace said softly, making way for Sara.

Grace's interest piqued when she saw the way Sara stared at Danny, and the way he stared at her too, and she smiled even more broadly as they hugged. She shared the same expression on her face with others, and guessed others are starting to catch on. She wished they could open up to the others, to all of them and make their relationship a thing to be relished before them, and as she watched, her mouth was agape in awe, her eyes wide with surprise and excitement, and she felt like screaming, if only screaming was her thing.

They started clapping, cheering and calling out Sara and Danny's name as they kissed, and at that moment, Grace wished that it was her and someone else.

Chapter Thirteen

It was half past 5:00 PM, and laughter and clinks of glass against another glass filled the air. The bar was boisterous, full of life, that anyone who came there would have no reason not to forget their worries. After all, drinking and sharing laughs seemed to be the reason for coming to the bar, at least, to the many folks that trooped in from time to time.

Grace and her crew had gone into the bar to celebrate Danny's new van, and their laughter was laced with the others around them, which made the whole place roaring with noise. Yet, it was this one exuberance all of them liked, to sit and drink over something that's actually worth it. For today, it was Danny and Sara.

"You took us by surprise, Danny boy. We weren't expecting this one, no, we weren't," said a voice filled with vigor and beer, his voice pushing against the faces of the others around him. He sat beside Danny and had his hand around Danny's neck. It made Danny a bit uncomfortable.

"Yes, Danny, I am quite happy for you, for buying a van of your own, finally, you do not have to walk or take the bus anymore," a baritone voice said to him. He had dark hair, shabby beards spread all over his face, and was a plump-looking figure. He wasn't fat but had a build that could pass as fat.

"Taking the bus can be fun sometimes, Jeff, there's nothing wrong about walking or taking the bus," Danny said to him, sounding convincing.

"That's quite right, Danny," Tom said as he turned to Danny in his flower-themed shirt, brown eyes, and square face.

"See? exactly my point," Danny said, looking at Jeff. His words were meant for Jeff, and Danny turned toward him so Jeff would know he was the one being addressed.

"Then again, nothing beats private transport," Tom said with a sly look on his face, his lips raised upward on his face and his brows arched in a pelting manner. Tom smiled as those words fell off his lips.

"Come on now, I thought you were on my side," Danny shot at Tom, wearing a shocked expression, but he isn't bothered by Tom's betrayal.

Everyone laughed, including Grace. She was having as much fun as the others did, and was happy she was there, with them and the glasses of beer that stood before them all. She didn't say much, there was no need for it. Though, she could talk, but she would rather have the others talk, than her to say something. So, she sat there, her white pearl earrings dangling beautifully on her ears, its white still visible under the dim, brown lights of the bar, her hair almost visible now as it has started to grow. She loved the part that was growing now, a new form of herself taking shape within her, a new wall building itself against the many things that may upset her. And so, she sat there, listening to the men chip at one another one person at a time, laughing at their jokes.

"Well, I can help you keep the van til you need it, or maybe when you are tired of walking of course," Jeff said, hitting Danny with his elbow in a sly manner.

Danny wasn't having it, but he thought it funny still. He shook his head, and said to them, "Well, if you don't know, walking can be a good thing for the human body and the environment. With all this thing about the earth dying and all, I think I may be doing the earth a favor."

"It is settled then! Danny doesn't want his van!"

"I didn't say that, Chris!" Danny spat out quickly, his face bright and cheerful.

The men laughed harder still. They were having fun messing with Danny's head, and it didn't help that Danny knew what they were doing, he simply played along, and night kept on going as smooth as they had all imagined. Still, Grace and Sara, the only two women in the group, said nothing.

"But, you just said you were doing the earth a favor, why turn back now? Need some motivation to continue?" Tom asked him, smiling really hard, he would cramp his muscles if he kept laughing. Soon, his face started to relax as he felt a little strain on his face, he moved his face this way and that just to feel himself again.

"I don't need your motivation, Tom, I am perfectly fine. And, I would like to keep my car, thank you." Danny said, content with his own words.

They all cheered and raised their glass cups in the air,

filling the atmosphere with the clinks of their glass cups, their smiles warm and radiant toward each other. Grace felt so wrapped up in their midst, so at ease that she didn't want to leave so early, to have it come to an end. It was a time she was bound to cherish for a while, to hold on to and look back whenever the memory presented itself. It was a period in her life that reminded her how much love people were willing to give.

"I have been thinking," Grace finally said something.

She had been quiet, a little too quiet, but fept relieved that the others went on, talking and laughing, without paying her much attention. She would often share glances with Sara, drink her beer and look at the faces with smiles and grins on them as teased Danny. But, that was it. That was all she did on the outside, but on the inside, her thoughts were a raging wave of a storm, knocking against her walls to break free. Such thoughts, a single line of it, was about to be shared, causing the others to fall silent.

"I was thinking, what made you both come out now?" she asked, "I thought, Sara, you and Danny were going to leave it till you all decide, did it come too soon."

Danny was stunned a bit, "How did she—"

"Actually," said Sara, stopping Danny short, "It came a bit too soon. Turns out Danny wanted us to let you guys know about us during the unveiling of the car, and I thought it was just perfect. Keeping your relationship from your friends can be…problematic at times." she further added.

"Well, it's nice both of you finally opened up about it.

I'm happy for you, both of you," Tom cheered, raising his glass to them.

"Same here. Though, I don't get why you had to keep it from us." Chris said.

Jeff interjected quickly, "Hey, let's just be glad they said it, and leave it at that, shall we?"

Grace smiled at Sara, " Sure."

***

Grace was now on her way to her sister's, and to her, the trip was a long one. Her sister lived a few miles from her, about 2-3 miles west from her neighborhood, and she wanted to drop by, to have a chat or two and see how her younger sister was doing. It has been a while.

She had a lot to think of after her time with her friends. She tried not to think about it as it often evoked certain memories, memories she wasn't so fond of. She would always protest against them, these memories of hers, whirling in her mind like an angry, raging gust of wind. Still, it comes back and she would try to shake it, but it would stick itself like gum under a chair or table. Grace hated it, she doesn't want this type of torture for herself. It wasn't what she wanted, to have to recall the moments she had once felt alive and wholesome. A time where she was ready to damn it all to hell. Now, her reality kept looking as though hell was manifesting.

Soon, the bus stopped at Crimson Avenue, a busy street with shops, restaurants, and various offices littered the whole place. People went about their lives, some going home, others still in their shops attending to their customers. They weren't ready to call it a day yet, not when the day hadn't come to a close.

It was almost nightfall, and the sky was now a pale blue and orange sheet of clouds, the sun was setting and the stars were starting to come into view. The dim blue sky brought with it soft cold winds, as Grace wrapped her hands around herself for warmth, walking briskly up the stairs that led to her sister's apartment.

She was fast, her mind distant but again, near. She wasn't looking as she trotted the concrete stairs in hurried steps, and hadn't noticed when a voice called out to her. She hadn't heard it the first time, but her ears came alive when she heard her name the second time.

"Grace!" the voice called out again.

She turned her head toward the voice, and her eyes brightened with awe and bemusement. She hadn't been expecting it, to see anyone she knew here and her tongue lay flat in her jaw unable to utter any word to the blue eyed, smiling red cheeks that stood behind her. It was Olivia again, and Grace didn't know what to make of their encounter here.

"Olivia! I didn't see you there, I am so sorry," Grace apologized, hoping to keep the momentum going.

"It is alright, Grace, you probably had a lot on your mind," Olivia expressed softly. Grace had always thought her to be quite thoughtful.

Grace had her arms crossed as she rubbed to make herself feel warm, "Yeah, it's this cold, I just want to get to a warmer place."

Olivia's eyes narrow with questions, "And where would that be? You have someone here."

Grace turned around, looking at a hallway behind her, "Ah, yes. I have a sister living here, a younger sister, and I have come to pay her a visit."

"Uhh, that's cool, I guess."

"Yeah."

An air of silence almost erupted between them, but Grace wasn't the one to waste much time. As the night came upon the city fully, the cold increased with a gradual intensity, though she was wearing a shirt, she still felt chills running down her body.

"Well, I will be on my way now, nice meeting you again, Olivia." Grace turned to go, but stopped and looked back.

"Hey, Grace," Olivia called, "I was thinking."

Grace watched her with rapt attention, listening to her every word, and wondered where she was going with it. Her face was neutral and showed no emotions, emotions Olivia might pick up and misinterpret. She wasn't really to explain herself or offset anyone. Grace didn't also want to make Olivia feel she had an interest in her, though she thought her to be interesting enough to have around. A conundrum she was still battling with. Yet, she stared at Olivia with a thoughtful expression, waiting for her to make her statement. The cold was gripling anyway.

"Yes?"

"I was thinking, can I get your mobile number?" Olivia asked, almost nervous and shaky in her voice, "I don't know if you can help me with it now, to call you next time."

Grace froze for a minute, then came back as though she had been knocked out of a trance, "Sure, sure…"

Grace brought out her mobile and called out the numbers for her. Olivia took it down in her mobile with a glint in her eyes, a faint smile appearing on her face. She had wanted to get Grace's number but couldn't as Grace had already gone out of earshot. She didn't bother still as she believed she would see Grace again, she knew her now and that was all that mattered.

"Got it!" Olivia said with a smile.

"Alright. I believe that will be all, and I will be seeing you next… heyyy," Grace said. She had just recognized someone coming up behind Olivia, and her face went up in a colorful flare of excitement.

"Heyyy, you finally decided to come," the lady's voice suddenly went flat, hitting Grace in the face like a brick.

Grace's face fell as flat as the words that had been uttered by her sister. She wasn't expecting a response like that from her, she had not imagined she wouldn't be as excited as she was seeing her. All Grace saw now was a cold, disinterested leaner figure with brown eyes that were tearing her down to size. It was an awkward moment for Grace, but Olivia seemed easier to handle than the cold figure staring right back at her, attempting to walk past.

"It is not what you think, Stephanie, I think you may

want to hear me out," Grace's voice faltered, her brows arched as she tried to convince Stephanie not to go into one of her bouts of rage.

"Hear you out? Please… you don't even stay that far from me, yet it took you two years to come visit your younger sister again!" Stephanie blurted out. She took a long look at Grace, heaving her chest in steadied breaths, she swallowed, then turned to Olivia, "I am so sorry, Olivia, I see you've met my sister." She apologized.

Stephanie seemed drained at the sight of Grace, and Grace knew she wouldn't be so pleased meeting her.

"Yeah, I have. I didn't know Grace had a sister," Olivia made an act to bring the two frigid sisters together, to make them feel a sense of care for one another. Being in the midst of two people having an argument or on the verge of it had a way of mixing up her feelings, which was why she would work to make them work it at the end.

"Yeah, 'had'" Stephanie emphasized, her troubled eyes fixed on Grace.

Grace had realized how much hurt she had caused Stephanie, she hadn't known not coming to check up on her would set off an explosion that would end up pushing her to the side, away from Stephanie. She hadn't known how long she had been away even, how long she hadn't spoken to her younger sister, only to show up on a cold Thursday night, dressed in a brown shirt and black trousers, her violin clasped in her hands, her feet stomping on the stairs as she moved up to go see her sister again.

What a fool she had been, to leave her sister like that, for such a lonely amount of time. The more she thought of it, the more her voice gave up on her. She was tired, but ready to make Stephanie see her as a sister again.

"Well, aren't you going to say anything?" asked Stephanie, who's now a stair higher than Olivia.

Grace hesitated, to the sight of her sister, she muttered, "I am sorry, Stephanie, but I can explain."

Stephanie didn't say anything, her throat was filled up and her tongue heavy with words. She only stared at Grace, who stared back with pleading eyes.

"Well now, I believe I will be on my way," Olivia said, taking the stairs down, "See you guys later, and hey, you are sisters, okay? No need to quarrel or be angry, we all make mistakes, please." She advised, her steps becoming distant the more she went down.

"How about we go inside, and talk again like sisters." Grace urged, her voice a husky tone.

Stephanie wore a faint smile, "I suppose so, lead the way. Hope you still know your way."

Grace grinned, "Of course, I do. I have a good memory, you know."

"Alright, I know… Hey? What's with the hair?" Olivia pointed at Grace's hair.

The little strands of hair now laid as a shadow on Grace's head, it made her appear even more gutsy than before.

"Oh, that? Uhh, it's just something I thought would look good on me." Grace lied, taking a turn to the right.

"Oh." Stephanie exclaimed, following Grace as they went through her apartment door.

Chapter Fourteen

Grace got home from Stephanie's place, exhausted. Her knees and calves throbbed, and her body felt too heavy for her to carry around. She trudged her way to her couch, slumping into it like a bag of potatoes. She felt like a bag of potatoes, and her mind only thought of how to get a good sleep for the night.

She leaned her head backward, her legs spread apart and her back in a form of lying position. She sighed, letting her muscles jerk and spread in relief, she sighed again. Grace closed her eyes, her eyelids burning a little bit as tears ran down her cheeks. She didn't think about it, she didn't feel it as the wet fluid found itself to the back of her head, that was the least of her concerns. She adjusted herself again, and let out a sigh, sinking deeper and deeper into the couch, letting her mind wander a little bit as she rested. And she sat there, recalling her moment with her sister, a smile rippled through her face.

Grace had just gone through Stephanie's door and into her living room. She remembered it and realized nothing much had changed, it was still the same two-bedroom apartment she had seen two years ago. Grace looked around, the living room still had white window blinds over the windows, the walls a brown coat of color.

Stephanie still had the set of brown couches she had bought more than five years ago, a small flat screen television that sat on a stand beside the wall near the entrance of the living room, the brown rug and the center table with a flower vase on it. Grace hadn't the slightest idea why Stephanie would want to keep a flower vase on the center table, it perplexed her but she said nothing of it.

Moments later, Stephanie walked into the room with two glass cups of fruit juice and some biscuits on a tray. She moved toward the table and dropped it on it. Grace looked at the cups and biscuits with a queer look, she narrowed her eyes at it and then to her sister. Stephanie noticed Grace's expression, but wasn't the one to admit to it, she knew why Grace had looked at her like that, yet, she feigned.

"What is it?" Stephanie asked in feigned confusion.

"Juice? Couldn't you bring something else?" Grace queried, sensing her sister only wanted to torture her.

"Let me see, you wanted me to go bring some whiskey or wine so you can take it?"

"Don't you want it, too? I hope it's not what I am thinking, Steph?"

Stephanie raised her voice slightly over the room, "What? That I brought these here for us on purpose? As a form of payback to all you have done?"

Grace replied, "Seems like it."

"Please, I only brought these because I have stopped drinking, and now live a more healthy life." Stephanie said, putting her back against the couch.

"Oh, I didn't realize that," Grace suddenly felt weak, she was

struck blind by Stephanie's revelation.

She had always known Stephanie was a bit like her, quiet most times, but can be fierce when enraged. And anytime she went through one of her moments of palpitations, she would drink, to drink away the heartburn she felt, toward another person who had caused the heartburn, the wrenching she felt in her chest. Alcohol was always the remedy for stuff like that, to numb the pain to the point of not having to feel it anymore, to cause it to come to a stop, that was the way Stephanie dealt with her problems. Which was also the same way Grace dealt with her own problems and heartburns.

Stephanie was also an occasional drinker, just like her, and was comfortable sitting down before a bottle of good whiskey or wine, and gulping down the content till the bottle had turned an empty shell of itself. Stephanie has stopped drinking? When was that? When did that happen? For how long? The questions ran a long line of clouds in Grace's mind, getting puffier and puffier the more she thought about it, but held herself from looking too stunned about it. She was happy for Stephanie, and that was all to it.

"For how long now?" Grace asked calmly, peering at Stephanie with caring eyes.

"Almost a year now," Stephanie said, taking a glass of juice to her lips, they were flat and pink and almost fitted quite well with her ruddy face, "You know, I was almost a goner once, I became so addicted to drinking, I couldn't help myself. I tried so hard to stop, I really did, but every single time, I would retract, my bum on the couch, and a bottle of alcohol in my hand, drinking myself to a pulp. It was a nightmare." she added softly.

Stephanie was almost speaking in a whisper, her words the same as the air she breathed, caressing Grace all over her face and her ears. Grace wasn't really happy she was hearing Stephanie was narrating this to her, it made her heart feel constricted, looking at her and know-

ing she wasn't there for her.

"I am sorry you went through all this, I should have been there," Grace said, going over to sit beside Stephanie.

"Yeah, you should have, but it wasn't your fault. I was so heartbroken, I drank so the pain could go away, to stop the bleeding that was pouring out of my heart. I didn't know I was killing myself."

She wanted it to stop, for Stephanie to stop narrating her story and just lay in her arms, consoling her like the big sister she should have been. The big sister she should have been years ago.

"It is alright now," Grace said, pulling Stephanie's small frame toward her, her head on Grace's breasts.

Grace stroked her hair as she tried to make Stephanie feel better, to let her know she cared, that she still cares. And would not abandon her like she did in the past. The two ladies sat quietly on the sofa, their thoughts spreading ever so thinly through their minds, pleased they were now beside one another.

Grace sighed again, pushing herself forward, in an upright position. She still had her trousers and shirt on, and hadn't made her take either one off. Her head throbbed a little, and she got up and trudged to her bedroom. She needed a bath, to have herself soaked in the tub as her body regained its normal self, and then enter the bedroom for some sleep.

She made it to her bedroom, and as she got to her bed, she started taking off her clothes one after the other till she was totally naked. She stretched her pale body, letting out a yawn, and with sleepy eyes, she trudged to the bathroom. When she had done all she could do in there, she climbed into the tub, and sighed a relief, sinking into the warm water.

"This is it," Grace said to herself, her head on the tub's frame, and her eyes shut, absorbing every ounce of warmth she could from the water.

Moments later, her phone started ringing. Grace heard, but decided she won't get it, the water was too good to leave, too good to climb out of for a phone call that could wait later. She sat there, and ignored as the call kept on coming in and her phone kept on ringing. Grace's face was writhe with growing frustration, her face wrinkled again when she heard the call, and again when she heard it the seventh time. She shot her eyes open and gave the ceiling a blank stare, her lips tight in a knot. She got out to see who it may be.

She got to her and stared at the screen of her smartphone, it was Olivia that had been calling, and Grace felt like dropping her phone, and going back to her tub. But then, she needed to know why she called so many times. The call came in again, and Grace picked.

"Hey, Olivia, sorry I didn't pick up the call earlier, I was in the bathroom." she lied, "Yeah … Yes, I am free tomorrow, what's wrong? … Ohhh, yeah, I think I can make out time for it, it shouldn't take much … Yes, so where is the venue … Okay, noted Olivia … I will be there by 8:00 PM, trust me … Alright now, good night."

Grace turned back and resumed her place in the tub. Her heart pounding steadily, her eyes shut, and her head on the tub's frame. She had a date with Olivia tomorrow, and a performance with her band. Not exactly the trajectory she wanted her life to follow, but however it may come, she was not going to let herself go this time.

"Finally, some quiet." Grace said.

***

The white of Grace's walls and furniture in her room shone bright and clear, a yellow patch on some of the surfaces and edges. The sun was already out and high above the sky, bringing with it the dawn of a new day.

An alarm clock goes off, a digital, rectangular device with a screen that showed the time sat on a bedside drawer and beeped Grace awake from her sleep. She mumbled and grumbled and flung her hand at the device till she was able to turn the beeping off. The clock stopped, but it seemed Grace wasn't ready to get out of bed yet. She laid still, under her blanket—a plain navy blue blanket—her body rising and falling, and with no sign of getting out of bed anytime soon.

As though waking from a nightmare, Grace jolted from her bed, her eyes wide open in terror, her mouth agape breathing heavily, she reached for her phone beside her and peered at it. 8:35 AM was the time she saw.

"Oh no! Isn't the gig today?!" she asked herself, "Oh my God, it is way past time, this is bad!" she panicked.

She dialed a number on her phone, and pressed it to her right ear. The phone rang through, and soon, a voice was heard at the other end.

"Hello, Grace, how are you?" a bubbling voice asked her, soft and soothing like the fresh scent of roses. Grace had always admired such a voice.

"Oh, Sara, I'm fine, how about you?" Grace replied,

maintaining a cool voice as possible as she could.

"I am good, Grace," Sara replied to her, "Are you coming for a little practice at the studio today? You know, for our gig this evening?" she asked.

Grace became bemused at what Sara said, "This evening?"

"Yes, Grace, this evening by 7:30. Have you forgotten?" Sara said with her voice coated with bewilderment.

Grace hesitated for a while, she could say a word, her eyes unblinking. She froze for a moment, then came back to herself, "No… no, no, no way I could forget. How would I forget? I totally remember it's this evening, and trust me, I will be there."

"Great. So, will you be coming in for practice?"

"I don't think so, Sara. I will just come by the studio when it is time to go. Yeah, that's what I will do."

"It's fine, Grace. We will be expecting you."

"I won't miss it."

Grace dropped the phone and fell back into her bed. She had panicked earlier, and still had more time to herself. Then, it struck her, a thought she had had lingering in her mind since yesterday. A date she remembered she was going to be at.

"Why does Hailey keep coming up?!" she asked herself. Grace, for the past few minutes, had been trying to remember who asked her out on a date the night before. She also hadn't the miniscule idea why she was finding it difficult to remember things this morning. She must have been stressed throughout yesterday, and must have slept herself to the point her mind is still taking its time gathering up her thoughts.

Tired and mentally drained, she sighed, and the thought of who asked her out the night before became clear to her. It was Olivia. She stared at the ceiling for minutes on end, her eyes roving all over it, thinking. Thinking of Hailey and what she would be doing at the moment.

It is 7:30 PM, and Grace is all set for her gig this Friday evening. She walked out of her apartment in a pale pink summer hat, a shirt and loose pants of the same color with a belt strapped around her waist. She held her violin case in her hands trotting downstairs, and up to the bus-stop to take the bus to the studio. She wouldn't be on bus 102 this time, it's past 7, and the operation of the bus had long passed. It didn't matter, Grace paid no attention to it.

She had taken the bus so she would be able to join her friends in Danny's van. He had promised to take them, and didn't want to be the one who spoils the fun for everyone.

Few minutes later, she alighted from the bus – bus 19 it was – her black heels doing some justice to the clothes she was wearing. She walked into the building that had the studio, and click-clacked her way to the second floor. She got to the door, and found her friends already packing up, getting ready to go.

Jeff looked up toward Grace, "Good! We are all here."

"Grace! Glad you could make it." Sara said, holding firm her cellophane so it doesn't fall.

"I told you I would be here, didn't I?"

Sara smiled, and gave her a hug.

Some minutes later, they were at the event. A small, yet lavish event that had all types of people in attendance. It was a small meet and greet for business people from around the country who had come for a good time together and networking. And who, strikingly, shared the same taste in soulful strings and keys of classical musical performance, and Grace and her team didn't fall short to entertain them all.

They had everyone dancing, on their toes, with their partners in their hands. Laughing and cheering, the music filling their hearts, mood, and mind with the right color-ful emotions they needed to interact with another. Most of them men wore suits, most of them black, and some blue, white, or grey, and the women wore beautiful gowns of white, emerald green, sky blue or even coal black. Dresses that shimmered and sparkled under the bright lights of the room they were in, smiling as bright and as cheerful as they all can.

As Grace played her violin, immersing herself in the long, pleasant sounds coming from the strings, she shut her eyes, listening to the rhythm and flow of the music they were all making. A moment later, the music started to come to an end, for the first half of the event. The ringing tune of the cellophane started to come to a slow stop, the airy strings of Danny's guitar soon started to wane as well, and the music they all made soon came to a stop. And as they had imagined, they stood with an expression of awe, all smiles and chests heaving, listening as the audience they had played for clapped, their claps rising to the ceiling and through the door behind them. The clap lasted for about two minutes, but that was the best two minutes of their lives.

And as they smiled and gasped with excitement, Grace was the only one not feeling too comfortable. She tried to cover it up with a smile of her own, but it appeared too difficult for her. Too difficult to keep her eyes from wandering, from wandering back to Hailey who stood in a lacy black dress and pearl necklace, clapping with the audience. Hailey's gaze was also on Grace, it was fixed on her and no one else. She had a faint, proud smile on her lips, and Grace saw her in a way she had never seen her before. Red lips, white teeth, a slightly made up face, and the dress clung to her exposing a somewhat hourglass figure. Grace was suddenly out of breath, and all she wanted was to leave the place.

Luckily, she did, and she was now where their things were. She was quiet, her emotions were muddled up and her head ached as her thoughts whirled in her like a storm. Her team had noticed, but thought it best to let her be. She wouldn't say much to them, and anything they asked, Grace would say stiffly and quickly, "I am perfectly fine, don't bother about me." And she would be left alone.

Soon, she made to leave. Her violin case clutched in her hand, she stomped on the floor in rigid steps toward the door.

"Hey, Grace, we aren't done yet, where are you going?" Sara cried.

"I need to go home." Grace replied in a mutter, her gaze on the floor as she walked briskly on her way out.

"Grace?" … "Grace, please stop." … "We haven't done it yet!"

They all said, but all Grace could say was, "I am sorry, I need to go."

On reaching the door knob, the door pulled open from outside, and Grace froze. A set of coffee-brown eyes stared at her now, and Grace felt like giving up, her body sprawling on the floor, beneath the person that was staring at her. It was Hailey, and she had a look that showed she wanted Grace to stay a bit longer.

"Hey, Grace." Hailey said warmly.

Grace's voice gave up on her, she tried to say something, but her tongue failed her, and she stood there, transfixed to a spot. She let out a sigh and finally made it to speak.

"Hello, Hailey."

Hailey smiled, it has been a while since she's heard Grace say her name. It made her skin tingle and a cold shiver rushed through her body. The right kind of cold shivers.

Chapter Fifteen

After her night at the event, and with Hailey, Grace got back home, feeling numb and her mind was once again a tempest of raging thoughts. Flashes of pictures and events had enough force to sink her deeper into her feelings like a muddy quicksand under a rainy sky.

She got home some few hours ago, dropping her violin near a couch in the living room, and slumping into the couch with a restless thud. The event got her exhausted, playing in front of many eyes all got her exhausted, but the most of it all was the sight of Hailey. Her mind hadn't been at peace since she knew Hailey was there, among the guests that came, she hadn't imagined that Hailey could ever be in such a place. And it bothered her to the point she nearly missed a string while performing on stage.

Grace curled herself on the couch, in a C-shape with her arms wrapped around her stomach. The incident had left her with a retching in her stomach and her heart burned anytime she recalled her and Hailey's moment.

"What was I thinking?" she said, wrapping her arms even tighter across her stomach.

Grace was flushed with a chill feeling when she saw Hailey at the entrance of the room they were in. So chill, she froze for a moment, her eyes weren't moving, her eyelids didn't blink, and not a muscle in her body moved. Only her chest rose and fell as she stood there, her gaze held with Hailey's.

Her mind tortured her, flashing into her pictures of Hailey's dress, her crystal earrings, her fine skin and oval-shaped face with red lips. She gaze at the red lips the most, they way they called out to her, to have her touch them and feel them as she had. It was a pure nightmare now Grace wasn't with her, she was by her side.

She turned again, "Why couldn't you tell her you were sorry?" she asked herself.

She could remember what she said to Hailey at the door, and anytime she did, her heart pricked her greatly that she curled inward on the couch, shutting her eyelids. It wasn't something she would have wanted to say.

"Why, Grace? you could have just said something other than 'Hello, Hailey,' you could have acted excited, but shocked to meet her. That would have made a difference. 'Hello, Hailey' was definitely not the best response to say." She said to herself.

Grace opened her eyes briefly, she had shut them too tight that it hurt her. She wanted to relieve them, to make them breathe again. Then, she shut them again, slightly now. She let her mind freely take over her.

"I loved your performance," Hailey said amidst difficult breath. She felt her heart constricting as well, she could breathe well and her

chest heaved just as Grace's did. Hailey wanted to leave, to walk out of there just as she had done some months back, but she couldn't. She tried to move, but her muscles froze too greatly for that.

Grace said nothing as well, she only thought of the moment she had shared with the red-lipped lady that stood before her, and how much she had missed it.

Hailey made to speak, turning toward the hallway and back to Grace again, "Err, I will be expecting your next performance. I am sure you will blow everyone away."

Hailey still didn't move from the entrance, and Grace still held her gaze. She couldn't hear anything else, Grace, she wouldn't know if her team found her situation strange and unfitting, and would have loved it if she talked with Hailey somewhere else. She knew they would be talking, whispering to one another, their minds trying to fathom what's happening, and for a moment, she wished someone could come and shake her back to life, to bring back her voice. She wanted to go closer to Hailey, to hold her face, but her emotions were too conflicted for that.

Hailey sighed, and Grace could see the forlorn in her expression.

"Hailey, wait," Grace said as Hailey made to leave.

She once again held Hailey's crystal clear eyes as it widened in glee.

Grace searched her mind for what to say, words that could clear the tension between them, and not bring back what she longed for but couldn't bring herself to desire it.

"Our performance will be better than the last." Grace said defiantly.

Hailey gave her a long look, and the forlorn on her face deepened. It sank deeper and deeper, like a stone cast into the ocean, and Hailey *wasn't sure if this stone could be resurfaced. Her worst fear had just manifested itself, and she blamed herself for it.*

Hailey swallowed, folding her lips into one another, licking it slightly, she could taste the bile her mouth had gathered, and she could feel her body turning to water. She left Grace without saying a word.

Grace laid on her back now, her eyes peering at the concrete ceiling, its white, a pale black, or more like grey as her living had no lights. Grace hadn't turned on the lights as she entered, she hadn't thought of it, and was fine with staying in the dark. An atmosphere that reminded how dark her world was.

She sighed.

"What about Jade?" she thought, but a beep on her phone stopped her midway.

A notification had come through her phone, and she made a very wild guess. She checked it, and made to reply back, albeit with sullen hands and fingers. It wasn't who she was expecting.

It was Olivia.

– "Hello, Grace, you stood me up! What happened?!"

Olivia sounded angry in her text, and Grace didn't have the mental energy to consider what she had done. Though, she knew she had failed Olivia but all of that meant nothing now.

Grace texted back, "I am sorry, Olivia. Wish I had called earlier, but there was a delay at the event I went to perform."

Grace lied. She was disinterested in what was happening but she still lied. It was the one thing she could do, to prevent Olivia from knowing what had actually stopped from coming to the date Olivia had arranged.

– "You went for a performance?! You should have told me!"

– "I forgot that as well. My apologies, Olivia."

– "Wow, Grace, how nice of you. I should definitely invite you over for another dinner, what do you think?"

Grace knew Olivia was being sarcastic. She tapped on her keypads to text her a reply.

– "Let me make it up to you, Olivia. Choose the time and place."
Grace waited for the reply. She could see the three dots down at Olivia's end of her messenger wall, meandering about to pop into a block of words.

– "Borna Art Gallery, around Freemill street. Tomorrow 8:00 PM. Don't be late!!"

– "I won't,"

Grace dropped the call, letting her phone fall with a thud to the ground, she fixed her eyes back at the ceiling, and with a heart filled with dull colors, she sighed. For that night, Grace slept on the couch, with Hailey being the last image she saw. And as she closed her eyes, she could see Hailey didn't seem too happy.

***

It was almost 7:00 PM, Grace had her yellow lights on, and it made her white-painted apartment and everything in it refreshing. It had a roomy atmosphere, full of air and elegance, a portrayal of Grace's personality. One of thoses days she was the one who she had envisioned herself to be – self-conscious and confident – and her gait was a shadow of that.

She got out of her apartment in a green, sparkling silk dress that showed her left thigh, and clung to her frame that revealed her shape in all places. She had her hair still low but a bit grown, crystal-studded dot earrings, and a white pearl necklace. Grace wasn't the one for make-ups, she hated the way it made her face feel, the tingling and smell and the way it stiffened on her face during hot periods. She had had her experiences and wasn't ready to go through it again.

So, today, Grace went out with a naked lipgloss on, and a face that screamed of good facial care and treatment. She sashayed her way to the garage under her apartment building, where her car, a blue convertible, was parked. She got into it, and sped off to the venue, Borna Art Gallery.

A few minutes later, she arrived at the gallery, at 8:15 PM, and went inside. Paintings of different kinds hung brilliantly on the wall, oozing bright, immersive colors to the eyes that beheld them. The gallery was a big one, with walls that were 10-12 meters high and over 12 pictures hung on it.

Grace walked around in the gallery, a tint of admiration for the art and paintings she was looking at, a faint smile ripping through her face. She looked at the art for some time before she realized she had come here for a meet up.

She put her hand into her purse and brought out her phone and gave a call to Olivia. When she was done, she waited for a moment, for Olivia to come get her.

She was looking at a painting when she felt a hand touch her. She turned back to meet the graceful eyes of Olivia, beaming at her with an evergreen smile on her face.

"Olivia! It's so nice to see you!" Grace expressed, accepting Olivia's hug.

Olivia moved back to face Grace, "It's so good to finally meet you, Grace. Lord, I thought you weren't going to show up again."

Grace smiled, slapping the air before her, "Not this time, I told you I was going to come, didn't I?"

"Yes, you did." Olivia smiled even more tenderly.

"Alright now, why have you decided that we come to an art gallery instead of a restaurant? Don't mind me, I'm just curious." Grace asked, her arms folded around her, staring at Olivia's twinkling eyes.

Olivia started to walk slowly within the room they were in. Grace walked beside her, trying as best as she could to listen.

"I have always loved art, Grace," Olivia revealed, glancing at the art paintings on the wall, "It is what reminds me that humans are still capable of beautiful things, creating something so creative with that many colors can only be done by someone who sees the colorful side of life. Don't you think so?" she asked Grace.

Grace stammered, trying to reply suitably, "Y-yes, absolutely. Surely, it takes…great attention to know what's beautiful and what's not."

"That's right, which is why I have called you here, to show you the wonders I love to behold." Olivia spread her hands apart to show Grace the paintings

Grace looked around, the mishmash of colors on canvas were indeed alluring to her. The styles and meanings the paintings conveyed, the way they stood out and spoke to you as they talked, Grace didn't say much but to look at them. Surreal theme imagery with strong lighting. She wanted to be alone there and surrendered to painting, that's how she liked to consume art.

"This one is one of my favorites, do you know what this one means, Grace?" Olivia asked as they approached a particular painting.

Grace said nothing at the moment, because she didn't like art to be interpreted. Instead, she looked at the yellow, green, black, and white colors stretched into something like a lean woman with straggly hair. She was on her knees and her back leaned backwards, about to touch the ground, one of her hands was on the ground and the other on her forehead. She had her mouth agape in a circle and tears were shown in her eyes and down her cheeks. There was another person in the painting, a figure of another woman, his back was turned to the woman and he seemed to be leaving as he was quite distant from the wailing woman.

Grace looked at it some more, and felt the pain.

"I believe the art is talking about a woman who got her

heart broken by her lover, and this here shows that she must have pleaded with her lover but she refused to take her back. Which was why she left, she just walked away." Olivia said softly.

Grace smiled with admiration. Olivia's face lit up with joy, and turned to the image again; "The art is simple but filled with emotions in it, that everytime I look at it, I imagine the hurt the woman in the art must be facing. Sometimes, when I come here, and I am before it, I stare at it for a very long time, often putting myself in her position."

Grace looked at Olivia's face, it was serious and somewhat sullen, as though she was going through her own heartbreak as well. Then, Olivia turned and met Grace staring at her, she smiled. Grace smiled too, before turning her gaze back to the art.

"Have you ever had your heart broken before?" Grace asked, almost unexpectedly.

Olivia laughed, a short laugh before turning to Grace. She still had her eyes fixed on the painting.

"Of course, I have. Many times." she replied, facing the painting again, "And there are times I wished I could go back and make things right, with the one I once loved." Olivia admitted, her words having more weight than it had ever had before.

Grace turned and looked at her, and all she saw was a woman who had her regrets, and would turn back the hands of time if she had the chance. She would go back, and make things right with whomever she had loved.

The moments Grace stared at her, Olivia didn't turn.

She still faced the painting, quiet and deep in her thoughts, waiting for someone to jerk her free. For someone to bring her back.

"Well, can't you still go back and make things right?" Grace knew Olivia had referred to someone, a person in her past relationships, but wasn't ready to make direct inferences.

"No, I don't think I will. I left things to rot way beyond repairs, even though she still came back, I let my insecure emotions get the best of me, and it ended up ruining me. So, no, the damage has already been done."

Grace's mind tingled with a feeling of having experienced something like this before, to have to see something you love go. She thought about it again and again, and the more the images came up in her mind, she was more convinced her story would soon be like that of Olivia's, and her heart went down to her stomach the moment she realized it.

"Could it still be possible?" she asked herself.

She stared at the painting, her mind reimagining the figures drawn with the stroke of a brush, taking them out and putting new figures in their place. She looked at it again, and in the wailing woman's place was her, Grace could see herself in it. She wasn't weeping, and she wasn't bent either, she was standing on her feet, her eyes to the ground, looking gloomy.

Another figure replaced the other woman, but this time in a dress and with her hands wrapped around her body. Grace knew this woman, wished she in the painting could move toward her, to hold her from walking away, but she couldn't and she hated it. Grace stood in the painting, unable to move toward the woman, and at that moment, her body felt a bit numb.

"Hailey."

Chapter Sixteen

Grace hadn't been sleeping too well lately. For days now, she had battled with her inner self, her own subconscious, pushing and shaking certain thoughts off her mind, running away from the possibility of actually having something. She feared these thoughts weren't what she wanted, so she pushed, and when it seemed it wouldn't go, she pushed even harder, lest it consumes her.

After her time with Olivia, at the art gallery, she had been restless the following day, and the days that came, she sank deeper into despair that she didn't go out throughout those days. She cut herself from interacting with anyone, she couldn't go out as much as she used to. She was so emotional grey that things and people seemed tasteless and colorless to her. She had even feared she was derailing into depression.

She got out of bed, groggy and with sunken eyes, she walked to her fridge in the kitchen to pick a wine bottle from it. She took it and brought out a cup to pour it in, and she paused. She didn't always drink her wine from a cup, she only did so when she had guests or was in the right state of mind, but not from a cup. But, that wasn't what stopped her. She had heard a door jam against its frame, its sound similar to one she had heard, and it made her memory relapse to the moment she had heard it.

It might have been sunny or cloudy, Grace couldn't tell. She heard a knock on the door and when she opened, she saw Hailey leaning in to kiss her. She could remember their conversation, the words she said, and the look on Hailey's face when she said it. She could also remember how Hailey left the house while she was in the kitchen getting their drink ready, how she had heard Hailey jam the door. It all felt real to her now, as though she could see it play out in front of her.

And, for a few minutes, she thought about her love for Hailey, and realized there was more to give and have if she had Hailey by her side. When she saw Hailey at the event, she could see the desires that were in her brown eyes, desires she had seen when they made love together in her dream. Those desires were still there, and they were begging to have her back.

Grace had decided that she would go for rehearsals today, at the studio. It is a fresh Tuesday afternoon, and she felt like she owned today and everything it had to bring with it. She walked down the sidewalks with a faint smile, a hat on her head and a white sweatpant and her favorite turtleneck, a red woven turtleneck with long sleeves.

The colors she had been seeing all around her before the dilemmas she had suffered had started to manifest itself again. She now saw everything in a different light, and was ready to make things work for her the way she wanted. She would no longer settle for compromise or hide behind whatever was right. She would go for what she believed in and wanted, and if it fails, she would leave it.

"Screw it all," was what she said standing in her kitchen,

a bottle in hand and a glass cup before her on the counter. She would later go on to screw it all.

Thirty minutes later, she was at the entrance of the building where the studio was, and a moment later, she entered through the door. She froze and all eyes were now on her.

"Come on, guys, this place is a mess!" she pointed out, albeit heartily.

"Grace! Good to see you again! Where have you been?!" Chris yelped, walking toward her.

"I have been around, Chris. I am fine, thank you." she replied, taking her violin out of its case.

Sara walked up to her and muttered with concern in her voice, "We were very worried about you, we thought you had traveled out of the country."

"I didn't go anywhere, Sara. As you can see for yourself, I am fine, really."

Sara glared at her thoughtfully, not convinced Grace was saying the truth, but had to let it be as she couldn't sense any discomfort in Grace's voice. Grace had always been great at it, masking her true feelings. But, this time, it was different, they only couldn't sense it.

"Okay, guys, we are now complete. Let's begin!" Danny urged them all.

For the next 30 minutes, the studio was filled with a mix of different instruments and sounds, lifting both heart and soul to its tip and making it expand all through the body.

Danny's hands on the strings of his guitar; Sara on the keys of her cello; Chris with his drums beating away to his heart's content; Jeff's fingers working on his saxophone creating airy rhythms that bounced smoothly off the walls; Tom with his piano, pressing melodically keys that blended with their song; and Grace capped it all with the slow flow of her violin. Everyone got into their zones and made magic with their fingers.

After their heart warming music, they paused for some interaction, like they always did after they were done playing. Grace sat on the couch, glancing at Tom pressing his phone. He had been like that since they were done playing, his eyes on the screen, tapping on it. He would let out a little laughter every 4-5 minutes, and Grace could see that Tom was a bit different now.

"That's odd, he would have been here trying to keep a conversation with me." Grace asked herself.

She got fed up and too curious to keep sitting down. She wanted to know what was up with Tom and be the one to initiate the chat this time.

"Hey," she said to him.

Tom took his head up to meet her, he smiled and said, "This is a surprise… Look who Grace is talking to, Me!"

Grace smiled with a feigned disinterest, "I'm sorry for ghosting all this while, I was just not feeling okay."

"That's fine, Grace. The most important thing is you're back now, and that's all that matters." Tom reassured.

Grace's face turned tender, she passed a tongue through her lips, "So, I have been seeing you all smiles, what's happening."

"Oh, it's—"

"Hey, Grace!" said Sara, breaking into Tom's words. Sara gasped, turning toward Tom, "I hope I didn't interrupt anything here?"

"No, you didn't. It's fine." Tom replied her.

"So, Grace, we were thinking, both I and Danny, if you could come to our house for a double date?" she asked, "Danny and I. You and…maybe Tom!" she shrieked.

Grace and Tom gave one another thoughtful looks, as though they were communicating their disapproval of the whole plan.

"I am sorry, Sara. I don't think I will be able to make it, I'm so sorry."

"Oh," Sara expressed sullenly, "Come on now, Grace, don't be a sourpuss, it will be fun."

"I actually have this thing I am—"

"Come on, Grace. Don't do this, just go."

Grace stared at Tom with a thoughtful face, then at Sara. She shriveled her face, and breathed out, "Okay. I will be there."

"Great!" Sara cheered with a grin, "I will be expecting

you two!" she said trotting off.

"What?!" chorused Grace and Tom.

***

Grace wouldn't go on a date with Tom. He knew this, and didn't push Grace into bringing him along. She had expected it, but she saw that Tom no longer wanted to be by her side. Tom no longer wanting her attention, she felt free from it, his words and knack for pressing on. And for the first time in a long while, she and Tom sat on the same couch, a few meters apart, casually talking about other things but her. She felt light in her chest, and her body flared with a feeling of being unhinged. Grace sighed.

Moments earlier, Grace had called Olivia to ask her if she was free for the night, and would be able to go as her plus one. Olivia was excited about it, and told Grace she would be at her place to pick her up. Grace had been indifferent toward Olivia agreeing, she had wanted Olivia to be busy and unable to come, but then, it didn't go as expected.

Grace got out of her apartment in a fine, straight white trouser that folded at her ankles, smooth to the touch was the fabric of the trouser, and she wore a loose leaf-themed, ash-grey shirt and black heels. She went outside, and saw Olivia was just pulling up the street with her car. Grace pulled the door and got in.

Olivia looked at her with an admiring gaze, "You look really great."

Grace turned to her, a faint smile on her face, "Thank you. Now, we need to go, else we will be late. It's almost 8:00 PM."

Olivia drove to Danny and Sara's place, and got there ten minutes later. Grace knocked on the door, and Sara showed up moments later, wearing a loose lime-green gown, light make-up with only lip gloss, and had her long blond hair tied to the back.

"Heyyy," Grace said with a grin on her face.

"Welcome, though you are late." Sara teased.

"I am sorry, we were held up by—"

"Oh, stop it. I was only messing with you, in fact, you are right on time." Sara said in a high-pitched tone. She then turned to Olivia who's smiling at her, "Errr, Grace, won't you introduce your friend to me?" she said, grinning at Grace.

"Oh!" Grace gasped, "Forgive me. Sara? This is Olivia. Olivia, Sara."

Olivia moved toward Sara, giving her a hug "Nice to meet you."

"Nice to meet you, too." Sara beamed, "Please, come in." she ushered them into the house.

Danny's place was located in a neighborhood a few kilometers away from where Grace and Olivia lived. It was a modern house made of wood and painted white with a pale black rooftop. This was Grace's first stepping into Danny's home, his living room was spectacularly magnificent to Grace. Partly due to his stereo system and music collections, he had a lot of her favorite records from Melody Gardot to Stacey Kent, and Diana Krall and Sarah

Vaughan. She gasped looking at them.

"That's a lot of music records." She said, "There are even some old time classics like Billie Holiday and Julie London! Sara, I will be taking some home, surely," Grace said to Sara as she sat on the couch.

"Well, I believe if Danny comes in, he may be able to arrange it." Sara said.

Grace looked around the room, "Where is Danny any-way?"

"Oh, he's upstairs, he will soon be joining us." Sara replied.

Few minutes later, they were seated round the dining table, everyone with a fork and a knife in hand, and a plate of stir-fry vegetables, chicken and boiled rice all placed beautifully before them.

"So, are you two like couples?" Sara asked.

Grace and Olivia glanced at each other for an awkward moment. They both didn't know the right answer to the question. Olivia looked at Grace queerly, waiting for Grace to say the words that were on her mind. But, Grace said nothing. Sara and Danny looked on for answers, anticipating what they would say.

Grace stammered, breaking the silence, "Ahh, n-n-not really, we aren't. We are…only friends. Yes, we are friends."

Olivia managed to keep a bright face after that, after Grace had denied their relationship, and what they shared.

Or, what she thought they shared. Grace, however, was nervous, yet unapologetic with her reply. She hadn't felt the same blossoming roses Olivia had felt, and had observed she was taking a liking to her, giving a reply of this nature would be doing Olivia a favor.

Sara couldn't see the strange, unpleasant tension in them. It was in the way they ate and the sudden silence that had gripped them both.

"I see…" Sara said, wanting to push the talk away. She had immediately started to regret asking that question.

The rest of the night went well, so it may seem. Grace and Olivia had put up a good act by constantly talking in a light-hearted way, laughing and throwing bants here and there. They even had Sara and Danny fooled, making them believe everything was okay.

However, Olivia is now certain she was never going to have a place in Grace's life, to have her as the one person who can share in her joy and happy moments, to create memories together. It was a bitter reality for her, one she had invested time, the dates, the calls, and texts, but above all, she was grateful for being in the know.

Chapter Seventeen

Hailey walked down the street of her neighborhood, taking in the evening breeze, it pushed up in her face with its cold touch. Winter was almost upon them, and the atmosphere was starting to get cold. It wasn't dark yet, but the sky was lit with a bright orange color as the sun set for the moon to take position for the night. People were seated on their front lawns, having chitchats over drinks, and the children played as though they couldn't be restrained. It was a peaceful evening for everyone, even for Hailey.

It was 6:15 PM, and Hailey had just closed from work, and was now on her way home, Jade's home. She and Jade lived together now, and had been together since Jade's break-up with Grace. Jade had forgiven her for it, and she had tried to maintain a good distance from Grace, though she still feels empty inside. She loved Jade and wanted the best for her lovelife with her, yet she felt she needed something else – someone else – Grace.

Hailey reached the front porch, a quaint-looking area, with chairs on the right and left corners, a table on the right, and a lightbulb above, on the ceiling. She walked into the house, and the smell of potatoes hit her nostrils, someone was cooking. She smiled and closed the door behind her, walking to the kitchen.

As she got nearer, the clanking of plates and spoons against one another got louder, and her lips widened even more in a smile. She got to the kitchen, and stared at Jade making a meal. Jade looked up at her, and smiled, putting her attention back on her cooking.

"You are back." Jade asked, stirring a paste in a translucent bowl.

"Yeah." Hailey replied, walking toward the counter where Jade stood, "That looks yummy, what are you making?"

"Apple pie, and some biscuits to go with it." she replied. She took the mix and turned it into a steel container. It got full and Jade started dressing it.

"That is going to taste really amazing." Hailey complimented.

Jade dressed the pie with a smile on her face, "You are just looking at it, wait till you have a taste."

Hailey beamed. Jade stopped dressing the cake and walked toward Hailey, wrapping her arms in a hook around her, staring passionately into her eyes.

"Now, how was your day?" Jade whispered to her.

Hailey's grin faded into a faint smile, looking at Grace with very thoughtful and searching eyes. She swallowed, and wrapped her arms around Hailey's neck.

"My day was fine. Thank you."
Jade leaned forward and placed a kiss on Hailey. She

closed her eyes as her head turned this way and that, driving Hailey closer and closer toward her. She had drawn Hailey so close their breasts and hips touched, and it seemed they were going to devour each other at any moment. Alas! Hailey pulled away, licking her lips softly with her gaze on Jade's face, she swallowed again, backpedaling out of the kitchen.

"Where are you going?" Jade asked.

"I want to freshen up, I will be right back."

"Alright, honey, the pie will soon be ready." Jade said loudly.

***

It is night time, and Hailey and Jade were in bed, wanting to sleep for the night. Hailey had already gone into bed, waiting for Jade to finish what she was doing and joined her. Hailey was lying on her back, her face up against the ceiling, recalling moments of the past and smiling faintly at it. It was one of the things she loved doing, letting her mind take her places she had before, giving her the nostalgic feeling that rushes through her body like a waterfall. And a few minutes before she slept, she replayed the moment she had met Grace, wishing they had said something better to each other, to spend some time talking other than that few minutes they stood staring at each other.

After a few minutes, Hailey waved the thought out of her head, and laid on her side. Jade had just come out of the bathroom after brushing her teeth for the night. Hailey was turned now, her eyes on Jade. She looked at Jade get under the sheets, leaning forward to give her a kiss. They kissed, a small smile on her face and her eyes gleaming in the dark room.

"Good night, honey." Jade said, adjusting the sheets over her.

"Good night." Hailey whispered.

Hailey was a bit restless tonight, she couldn't sleep no matter how many times she tried. She watched as Jade closed her eyes, almost about to sleep, she watched as she laid face up to the ceiling, her hands laced together under the bedspread, her body rising and falling in steady breath. Hailey thought it to be peaceful, Jade's sleep, devoid of whatever troubling thoughts that she may have. But, Jade wasn't asleep yet, Hailey knew this. She would be, but not yet.

"Hey? You asleep yet?" Hailey asked calmly.

"I am trying to." Jade replied with her eyes closed.

Hailey hesitated, "I was thinking, do you ever think that you've made a decision that turned out to be bad even though you thought it was for the best?"

Jade opened her eyes filled with thoughts, she was quiet for a while, thinking of a response. She hadn't thought of something like this before, and found it strange that Hailey would be asking her a question such as this.

Jade sighed, and turned toward Hailey, "I believe so. We all make bad decisions, don't we? Even when we thought it was going to help us in the long term, only for it to come back and bite us in the butt. It is just one of those things you can't avoid."

Hailey stared at Jade with intent, "Have you made a decision you are regretting now?" she asked.

"Not that I can think of, what about you?"

Hailey didn't know what her reply would be. She had a few decisions she had made in the past that have kept her awake most of the night. Decisions she ended up regretting, but she thought it was normal for people to make decisions such as the ones she had made.

Jade was still looking at her for a reply. She looked back at her, and nodded her reply. Jade gave her a long, penetrating stare.

"It's completely normal, Hailey. Now, go to sleep." Jade said to her.

Hailey did so. A few hours later, she came out of the bathroom and found that Jade's phone was on. She went close to it, and found that someone had sent a text to her. She looked closely and her heart wrenched and twisted in her chest, she looked at Jade sleeping face and doubted what she had seen. She decided she wouldn't say anything at the moment, walking to the side of the bed where she would sleep, slipping under the sheets.

A moment later, she heard Jade's phone ring, and had a wild guess who might be calling, she stayed listening to it. It rang again, and Jade moved on the bed. She awoke from sleep and stopped the phone from ringing any further. Then, got out of bed, and walked out of the room.

Hailey turned toward the door Jade had followed, her eyes misty with pain, she laid in bed with a burning in her eyes and throat, and a pounding heart that was hammering so hard she felt her chest would break open. When she couldn't take it anymore, she got out of bed, walking out of the room as well.

Hailey went downstairs, walking as slow as she could, stepping on the floor as light as she could. She could hear Jade's voice from the kitchen, and she didn't want her to know she was approaching. Hailey got to the kitchen and stood at the entrance, Jade's back was turned to her, holding a kitchen counter. Hailey could see she was talking to someone.

She watched as Jade spoke, the smile on her face, the change in her voice, the reassuring words.

"I don't think it should be that bad, baby. Come on now, go to sleep, it's quite late … I am going to hang up on you … Alright, since you can't sleep, picture me kissing you to sleep, placing soft kisses on your neck, hands, and face, holding you tightly to my body. Yes, picture that … Sure, I will come over soon … Alright, baby, see you tomorrow."

Jade dropped the call, and Hailey could see she still had a smile on her face, though she couldn't see it yet. Hailey watched as Jade turned and froze like ice, the feeling of being caught in the act choking her in the jugular. Jade said nothing, she couldn't even if she tried, she stood there, fear-gripped and white in the face with shame, staring as tears flowed down Hailey's face.

Hailey bit her lips as she swallowed with pain in her throat, "For how long has this been going on?" she asked with a brittled voice.
"Hailey–"

"I asked, how long has this been going on?!" she cried out.

Jade walked toward Hailey, "Hailey, please, listen to me."

Hailey wiped a tear that had flowed down her face, "After all I have done for you… for us… for our relationship."

"Please, listen to me. I can't explain all this," she said, getting closer to Jade, stretching her hand to hold Hailey. Hailey didn't resist, pain has made her body too weak to react, too numb to move. She stood watching as Jade took both of her hands into hers, their eyes communicating deeper emotions than it had since they have been together.

"Yeah, of course, you can." Hailey pulled herself away from Jade, "I will be going to bed."

Hailey went upstairs, her steps slow and painful, and her mind a furor of densed, raging thoughts. As she climbed, she paid no attention to Jade's voice as she called out to her.

Chapter Eighteen

Grace's morning seemed to be going great. She was listening to a song by Kaye Ballard. She danced to the song from the moment she put on, in a big shirt that closed in on her thighs, wearing a pair of socks with multiple colors. The song was loud, and Grace danced dramatically with almost everything in her room, from a vacuum cleaner, to the plate and pans she used in cooking, *Kaye Ballard* songs had always had a way to make her mood the color of rainbows.

Fly me to the moon
Let me play up there with those stars
Let me see what spring is like on Jupiter and Mars
In other words, hold my hand
In other words, baby, kiss me

She was still in her baggy shirt, it made her look like she was wearing a short gown, going about her apartment, getting things ready for the day.

Her phone rang and she walked briskly to the living room where she kept it. She peered at the screen and found it was Stephanie calling, she beamed and picked it up.

"Good morning, Stephanie, how are you doing?" Grace asked, walking back to the kitchen with the phone pressed to her ear.

"I am fine, and you?" Stephanie replied.

Grace put her phone in-between her ear and her shoulder, stirring her scrambled eggs in the pan, "Yeah, I am good, really good. Is anything the matter?"

"Oh yeah, but not in a bad way though, I just wanted to tell you that I have gotten another job!" Stephanie shrieked at the other end of the phone, sounding excited.

Grace wore a proud smile, "That's great news, Steph! I am really happy for you."

"Thank you, my lovely! I just can't wait to resume tomorrow, it's a really big role, with a big paycheck!"

"Woah, that's nice. But, in which company were you hired?"

"I, you sister, have been hired as a product manager!," she spoke with great relief.

"That's really nice, Steph, you deserve every little bit of what you are getting. I am proud of you." Grace's words bore more weight in care toward her sister than it had ever had toward anybody else.

"Thank you, big sis." Stephanie said, "So, have you gone to meet them? You know—"

"Yeah," she replied, serving the eggs on a plate, "I am actually getting ready as it is, I am just about to take my breakfast right now."

"Alright, Grace, I guess we will talk later then."

"Yes, Stephanie, we will. Once again, I am happy for you, always."

"I know." She hung up.

Few hours later, Grace got ready and dressed in a pair of blue jean pants and a long sleeve, button-up shirt, and a white sneaker. Her hair had grown into a short tuft that's just above her neck.

She was now on her way to visit Jade where she works, a decision she had made the night before. Grace wanted to patch things up with Jade, to talk to her and make things. Though she felt Jade may still be angry, she went anyway.

She felt she could conquer this day, and so she went on with her plans, and made her way to Jade's workplace, which is about 30 minutes away from her place when taking a bus.

Few minutes later, she arrived at the building, a small company where Jade worked as an assistant to the CEO. She got into the building, and greeted the doorman who stood in his green and red uniform, smiling at him. Grace took the elevator up to the 4th floor where she knew Jade stayed, an office where all the assistants stayed to do their work when they weren't with their boss.

She got to the office after a few steps to the right, and she stood, looking at Jade and her colleagues chatting. One of Jade's colleagues spotted her, and alerted Jade of her presence. Jade turned, sat still for a moment, her gaze fixed on Grace's soulful face. She smiled at Jade, but she only kept a straight face and did not smile at her back. She got up and walked toward Grace, stopping a few inches away from her, hesitating to say a word. Jade sighed, and walked toward a hallway, Grace followed closely.

"Jade, wait," Grace called out, treading behind her.

"What are you doing here, Grace? I thought we were through," Jade said, pausing in her steps.

"I know, and I am sorry." Grace apologized.

Jade and Grace paused, staring at one another for a frozen amount of time. All they could hear were muffled sounds around them, and the most audible of all were their breath as their chests heaved.

"I am sorry for what I did, and I hope you can forgive me for me."

Jade's thoughts were conflicted, unsure of what to decide or say. She could recall how she felt when she found out Hailey was cheating on her with Grace, and she trusted Grace, though she wouldn't do anything to hurt her. She had believed Grace was incapable of making her hurt, she was the first person she had ever felt so comfortable with, ever since they met in their freshman year at the university. Grace had always been that backbone that's always ready to support, no matter how withdrawn she could get, Jade knew Grace would always be there for her.

Then, she realized Grace, a friend she had trusted and confided in for years, was having feelings towards her girlfriend. She felt betrayed.

"And why should I? Why should I let a traitor like you back into my life?" Jade quipped.

Grace pulled back, "I don't know. And I will understand if you don't want us to be friends again, I was only hoping we could start off from where we stopped."

Jade's lips went dry and tight, she passed a tongue in-between them, she wasn't wearing lipstick, and just like Grace, makeup disturbed her to a great deal. Jade stared at Grace's with disheveled eyes, pacing around the hallway, searching for what to say. She came back to where Grace was, and faced her again.

"You know what, it doesn't matter anymore. None of it does, do you know why?"

Grace didn't reply.

Jade stammered, "Because… I and… I and Hailey aren't together anymore."

Grace's body flushed with indifference, hearing the news of a break-up and thinking what must have led to it. She wanted to ask, but held herself from doing it. Suddenly, her mind was now flooded with the thoughts of Hailey, the brown eyes, the gleaming teeth, her soft hands and her touch, all of it covered her mind faster than she could stop them. 'Jade and Hailey are no longer dating?!' she thought.

"Why? What happened?"

"She… she didn't state her reason, she just left."

Jade had an uneasy face, almost as though she was tense, though not fearful or angry. Grace couldn't notice it, and

Jade looked at her to see if she noticed anything, and was a bit relaxed when Grace showed no doubt written on her face.

"I'm so sorry, Jade. If there was anything I could do, I would."

"It's alright, Grace, I understand." Jade said, "And, I forgive you, for everything. We are good now."

Grace was awashed with gratitude, she left a lot lighter than she had ever felt, like a rock pulled up from her heart or her body. She felt glad that Jade had finally agreed to have her back as her friend, to come back and relive those moments she had once shared with her. On some days, she would imagine she and Jade sitting on the couch, a cigarette in-between their lips, talking about things they had done while they were apart, laughing at some of it.

This day, standing before Jade in a company's hallway, the picture of that happening was ever more glaring.

"Thank you." Grace whispered.

Jade still had an uneasy look, nodding softly at Grace's words. She started to feel she had stayed far too long with Grace and needed to go back into the office.

"Well, Grace, I will be going back now, talk to you later?" Jade said as she walked back, wearing a smile.

"Absolutely. I will call you."

Grace's day, as she had felt, did go as she had planned. And she felt even better now she knows Jade is a friend she can always call. Yet, her task was far from over.

Chapter Nineteen

Grace walked with a much slower step than normal, she had her arms wrapped around her body, a distant look on her face, staggering as she walked. She wasn't concentrating on the road or the people on it, she could see them but couldn't make out what they looked like or sounded like. It was as though her vision was hazy that afternoon.

The sun was out, and its light sent warmth down the city, relieving others of the burden of wearing thick clothes due to the cold. Grace, when walking under the sun, would concentrate on its rays and mentally hug the sun as it kissed her radiant face, feeling the warm touch it was giving her. But, her visit to Jade had numbed that feeling for her, she longer felt it and she walked down the street, on her way to a coffee shop, lost in a big pile of flashing images in her mind.

She took another bus, to where the coffee shop was, and she sat with a mien and heart that was weighed down by convoluted thoughts. Her stomach would rise and fall, and then rise again, a faint smile would then appear on her face and a moment later, the smile is gone. She stared out of the bus' window for some minutes of relief, looking at the passing environment outside, watching as they backpedaled backward as the bus went forward.

Grace thought looking at the people and buildings outside, it would bring a form of peace to her mind, dispersing into mist the thoughts clouding it. But, it didn't work, if anything, it only made it worse, and she wished she was with her headphones, it would have made a difference for her.

She sighed with a disgruntled voice, bruised and conflicted, she closed her eyes till she had reached her destination.

A moment later, her eyes opened to see she was almost there, and her chest tightened, a wave of cold shivers flushed through her body, and she breathed out a sigh.

The bus stopped, and she came down. She walked a few steps to the coffee shop, gripped with anxiety and fear. She clenched her fists, and went back a few times but kept convincing herself she needed to do it, and she would walk back to the coffee shop again.

"What if she's not there?... What will I do then?... What if she stopped working there? Arghhh, what am I going to do?" Grace thought to herself.

Grace was undecided, her head ached with the constant thinking, and when she couldn't take it anymore, she walked to the coffee shop with all the courage she could muster, and went through its doors. Grace moistened her lips with her tongue, searching around for her. But, I couldn't after a while. She turned to leave.

"Grace!"
Grace's stomach fell at the familiar voice, she paused holding the door, and hesitated to turn.

"Grace, is that you?" the voice said again.

With a stiff chest and the ground shaking beneath her, Grace turned toward the voice, looking over her shoulder slowly. Her eyes soon met the pale brown eyes she had seen at the event, wearing a black dress, red lipstick and a face that glowed with candor. A face she had touched and felt, and had fallen in love with.

She stood there, transfixed at a spot, gazing at Hailey as Hailey gazed at her back. Hailey seemed a little bit unsure if to hold her smile or not as her lips kept spreading and shrinking on her face. Grace noticed, and she smiled at her. Hailey smiled back even more, stifling a laugh, her white teeth gleaming under the afternoon brightness. It was such a beautiful sight for Grace.

She left the door, and walked up to Hailey. Hailey didn't move, her eyes glinted and searched Grace's face, and Grace could see Hailey had the face she had seen when she said "sip it" to her, or in the waiting room of the hospital Grace had taken Jade to. And it fascinated her even more.

They didn't speak for a moment, drawing the attention of people around them. Grace and Hailey didn't care about the stares or side-talks, they only cared about the unspoken words in their feelings, in their eyes, and their moment. And, for the time they stood looking at one another, they felt like touching each other so wildly, it would seem their feelings were untamed.

"I thought I would never see you again." Hailey said with a whisper, her voice had gone husky on her.

"No, I'm here now." Grace whispered back.

Hailey's eyes were growing stormy with deep emotions, and she felt like crying, Grace too, but she held it in. Hailey stifled a laugh, and wiped her tears. Grace laughed with her. They felt their spark once again, like a fire brought back to life.

"Come and sit."

Hailey pointed to a bench where they could sit and talk, and Grace followed behind.

"What about your customers? Who's going to serve them?" Grace showed her concern.

Hailey waved her hand at Grace's words, "It's alright, really, there are other workers here who can help me out. Besides, I am the manager now."

Grace howled at the news. She was filled with excitement. She beamed, "So happy to hear that."

"Thank you." Hailey said softly, her eyes sinking deeper and deeper into Grace's.

A silence befell them, both of them still beaming with looks loud enough for them to hear. Outside, the day was almost coming to a close, it was past 4:00 PM, and the cold was starting to come back. Hailey wore thicker clothes, a sweatshirt, and a scarf around her neck, and Grace wore something lighter, clothes that won't be fit for the cold, but that didn't matter at the moment. None of it did.

"I went to see Jade today, at the office." Grace broke the silence.
"Oh, that's nice." Hailey said.

Grace looked at her with intent, Hailey looked happier than she had been.

"So you heard about me and Jade›s breakup?"

"Yes, she had told me. She said you just walked away!"

Hailey's eyes fell on the menu on the table, looking at the words and numbers on it, but not paying attention. She was thinking of what to say.

She folded her lips a little bit, "Well… apparently she could cheat on me, it was going on for over six months, Grace!"

Hailey went silent again, oblivious to the rising angst in Grace. Hailey's words had evoked a storm of thoughts in her.

"And, the girl she cheated on me with," she said, bringing Grace's attention back to her, "is someone I have seen, another close friend of Jade's. Weird, right?"

Grace knew what she was talking about, and she felt silly for a moment. She asked herself why she had brought herself to such a situation, to love her close friend's girlfriend. Grace furrowed her brows at the thought, trying to make sense out of it all.

"Yeah, the strangest thing you will ever hear."

Hailey laughed, "It's alright, I actually don't feel too bad about it. For one, I feel much happier now, and since I am alone."

Grace held her gaze, watched as she said every word

without taking her eyes off her. She felt as though she could see the unspoken words in the way Hailey looked at her, the way Hailey smiled, and the way she spoke. There were many things going on in her mind, all at once, and it made her head ache.

"So, what are you going to do now?" Grace asked.

Hailey let out a sign, "I will be traveling out of the country, for some time. I just want to unburden myself a little bit, find myself again, you know what I am saying?"

"I do, Hailey. You definitely need it." She said with a fake smile.

It hurt to hear those words, of Hailey traveling to another country. She was happy, yet wanted her to stay, to still be around, in the coffee shop. She would have loved to come and see her, over a cup of coffee, to chat and laugh, to start off from where they had stopped, to undo the damages.

But, as she looked at Hailey, her timid, tender face ever more captivating to her, Grace felt Hailey needed to go. She needed to be alone as she had said, free from her. Grace thought it would be the best to let Hailey be, and be out of her life. It might have been a mistake from the beginning, her greatest undoing. If letting her go was the penance she would suffer, she would be ready for it.

Grace sighed, then she looked up, meeting Hailey's piercing eyes. Hailey had placed her hand on hers, and Grace could feel a rushing sensation pump through her. It was so surreal, something she thought would never happen, Hailey holding her again, the soft pads of her hand pressed against her skin. Grace's fantasies started to come alive again.

"I will miss you." Grace whispered.

"I will miss you, too." Hailey said to her.

Grace was on the brink of tears, though she held them back, Hailey was already tearing up, and the two longed for each other again, just as they had the last time they met. Outside was already getting dark, shops had started turning up their lights, illuminating the pathways and roads that laid by the side. The coffee shop lights were turned on, bright for the people in it, but the brightest light that shone was that emanating from the two women that stared longingly at each other.

***

Grace got home with more muddled feelings than ever, a mixture of affection and hate hitting her at the same time. She battled with separating them from her, to be free from them, yet it kept coming back.

She had left Hailey's place a few minutes ago, and was now home on her couch with a bottle of wine beside, a glass cup in hand, and a cigarette in another. Things she believed would bring relief to her, to help her numb the pain in her chest.

Her mind had been replaying what Hailey had said, about Jade cheating on her, and Grace felt she should have acquiesced to Hailey's request of loving her. Grace felt she had made a mistake, and whatever decision she was contemplating suddenly fizzled away with this realization.

With every drag at her cigarette, every gulp of wine she

took, her heart kept on skipping whenever the thought of Hailey flew past, with every beat harder and more wholesome than the last.

Her attention was soon averted to a knock on the door, and she got up to go answer it.

She opened the door, and saw Olivia standing there with a long creamy shirt, a scarf over her face and a quaint eyeglass over her eyes.

"Olivia," Grace called, "Please, come in."

"Thank you. " Olivia said, stepping into the immaculately minimalist abode of Grace, "You have a nice place."

Grace looked around her place, leading Olivia into her living room, "Thank you. Please, sit."

Olivia sat on a couch beside Grace, acting a bit disturbed, but kept it from showing on her.

"Do you want some?" Grace asked, offering her some wine and a cigarette.

"Absolutely."

Grace walked to the kitchen, and came back moments later with a glass cup. She turned some wine for Olivia and lit a cigarette for her. Olivia drew at it, and puffed the smoke into the air. It made Grace grin a little.

They sat in silence a little, Grace looking at her flat screen TV, and Olivia with an uneasy look. Soon, Olivia went closer to Grace, sitting beside her. Grace noticed, but only smiled.

"Grace," Olivia called, turning toward Grace, "I have something to ask you."

"What is it?"

"Have you ever loved someone, but felt the person won't love you as much as you did?"

This gave Grace something to think about. She paused on her drink and cigarette, and stared at the floor for a moment, searching her mind for an answer. She stared back at Olivia.

"No, not that I can think of, sorry."

"Well, I love someone, but I feel the person doesn't love as much as I did, and it scares me."

Olivia sounded bruised in her voice. It came out slow, almost painful, and Grace saw she wasn't feeling fine.

"That happens to many of us, Olivia, and I can give instances of many others that it has happened to, and you will see you are not alone." she reassuringly, "But, have you opened up to the person?"

"I want to ask, but I don't know what she will say."

"Fear. It can be very limiting if you have it in you. Olivia, take that bold step and say it to her...or him. Don't keep yourself in a box, don't do what I did." She encouraged her.

Olivia stayed quiet, her brooding face sinking even deeper, she wasn't sure of what to say, or bring forth what's really on her mind. She was gripped on the tongue, she couldn't move it, and this churned her stomach very badly.

"What if I told you you know this person, the lady I like so much,"

"That's even better, I can help you convince her. Who is she, anyway?" Grace paused.

"No, it's you, Grace. It has always been you."

It hit Grace, Olivia's words, resounding in her ears. She had always expected it, Olivia telling her about her feelings, and knew she was the one Olivia was referring to. But, she decided to play dumb and see where it leads. And it turned out to be what she feared. Grace didn't have a word to say to her.
"As I expected, you are not saying anything."

"It is not like that, Olivia."

"How is it, then? I thought we could share something together, to build ourselves in ways we wanted. I have gone nights thinking about you, being fascinated by you. But, all of that was useless, and had always been."

"Olivia, please, it is just that–" Grace paused, she felt Olivia was too hurt to hear she never took her the same way she did.

"It's alright, Grace," she said, taking in one gulp the wine in her cup, her face shrunk at the sharp taste. She stood to her feet.
Grace followed her as she stood up. She felt numb and unsure of what to do. She watched as Olivia dropped the glass, her eyes heavy with pain in them.

"I am so sorry, Olivia."

Olivia sighed, "Good night, Grace."

Grace watched Olivia leave her apartment, staring at the door she had gone through, keeping her gaze on it as though Olivia would come back and tell her she had been joking, but as minutes went by, Olivia didn't open the door again.

Grace slumped into her couch, thinking of how different she would have wanted her relationship with Olivia to turn out. Her night had been disturbed again.

Chapter Twenty

Jade had felt hurt when Hailey decided to quit their re-lationship, to walk away from her. She watched as Hailey turned her back on her and walked through the door. Jade's feeling dampened, and went dull. But, she had thought she wouldn't need Hailey in her life, to miss her that much, she saw no use in brooding over Hailey's absence, she had got another lover, and that should count for something, Jade had thought.

She woke up in the morning, and turned, extending her arm to where Hailey slept. The horror on her face when she saw the space empty, there was no sign of Hailey. She sighed and got out of bed, her mind growing foggy and hazy with only Hailey in sight. She decided to push it all away by calling her new girlfriend, to give herself some-thing to be thankful for and to brighten up the dull spaces in her. She had thought a phone call to her new lover would fix that.

She placed the call and it rang, and soon, someone was speaking on the other side.

"Hey, baby, how are you doing?" the voice on the other end asked.

"I am fine, Maria, just feeling a bit fuzzy this morning." Jade complained.

"Oh," Maria's voice sank, "Might be one of those bad days that just pops up in our lives. You will get through it, baby, I know you will."

"I hope so, sweetheart. I said I should call, I wanted something to make me feel better."

"That's so sweet of you, Jade." Maria gushed, "Okay, don't worry, I will come by your place after work, and I will calm your nerves, you hear me, baby?"

Jade robbed her forehead, a faint smile on her face, "Sure, I will be expecting that."

"Great, honey. Alright, I have to go now. I will call later, okay?"

"Alright."

Jade dropped the call, and plunged her face into her palms, and growled. She wiped it, and made to start her day without thinking of Hailey, filling her mind instead with Maria, an antidote to the venom that is Hailey, she thought. She had a hard time concentrating on her job, leaving herself to get distracted with the thoughts in her head. Things that happened around her didn't bother or affect her, even when a co-worker made a jeering remark at her, causing others to laugh at her, Jade didn't react. She only put up an injured smile, and walked away. Her co-workers looked at her, dismayed that they had done something terrible.

She was in the office, getting work ready for her boss, her

phone rang and she picked it up. It was Maria.

"Hello," she answered.
"Hey, love, how are you doing? Feeling a little better now?"

"Yes, I guess."

"Okay, what would you want me to get while coming?"

Jade leaned back into her chair.

"I don't know, Hailey, whatever you think is good."

"I am not Hailey, Jade. It's me, Maria."

Jade jerked on her seat, she could feel the weight of her body increasing and cold swirling inside of her.

She stammered, "I-I-I am sorry, Maria, it is not what you think," she said quickly, her voice was strained and painful.

"Whatever, Hailey. You need to get over her, she's gone already, stop your mulling, would you?"

Jade shook her head, stroking it with her right hand, the phone on her left, "I will, baby, won't happen again."

"It better not, jeez. I will be coming over to your place, and make you forget all about Hailey, I know you will like that, right?" she asked over the phone.

"I will, baby. Can't wait." Jade managed to say, smiling.

Jade dropped the call and collapsed on her desk. She

needed someone to talk to, but no one was there. She couldn't go to Maria as she felt Maria wouldn't understand. It was a crisis she didn't know how to handle.

Her head jolted up to a realization that popped into her head, she had one person, Grace. 'She would understand,' Jade thought, and she went to the house after work hours.

***

Jade was in her car, a small sedan she had bought when Grace convinced her to buy it, during the times their relationship was still as roses as it could be. She couldn't imagine telling anyone else of what she felt, how she felt it, and had known Grace would be the one to understand her more.

She couldn't run to Hailey, she wouldn't want to have her back even if she begged for her. She had always felt Hailey wasn't entirely in love with her, even though she showed it. Jade believed Hailey didn't love her as much as she loved Grace, and it made her look elsewhere for a form of love she could hold whole in her palms.

Few minutes later, she was parked outside of Grace's apartment building, and got out feeling an exuberance in her bones about seeing Grace. She walked to her doorstep, and gave it a knock. No answer, she thought it normal and gave it another knock. Few moments later, the door came open, and Grace stood before her in a tight sporty short that hugged her thighs and a green sweatshirt. Jade smiled and admired Grace's shape for a moment. Grace didn't smile.

"Hey, Grace." Jade said with a grin, an awkward grin, like she knew Grace could read her mind. She started shaking at the thought of it.

"You can come inside." Grace didn't look too happy, and Jade couldn't make out why.

She followed her into her apartment, walking quickly with a mixture of confusion and pain, the hem of her suit shirt flapping against her waist as the buttons were undone.

"What is wrong, Grace? Is anything the matter?" Jade asked, standing above her as Grace stood before.

Grace said nothing, she stayed quiet. She was distressed and troubled, and Jade got even more confused.

"And to think I came here to speak with you," Jade complained, throwing her hands in the air.

"What if I do not want to speak with you, Jade?" Grace whispered.

Jade paused, gripped by the words from Grace's lips. She had her hands on her waist, and a face that was restless. She was stressed already, she felt it, and Grace saying she didn't want to talk threw her into a void she was struggling to pull herself out from.

"That's nonsense… that's nonsense… why would you say–"

"Why did you lie to me?" Grace cut her off with a stiff question.

"Good Lord, what are you talking about, Grace?" Jade went over to sit beside her.

Grace didn't turn her gaze toward her, she was reluctant,

unwilling, and felt a furious need to walk away, away from Jade.

"Why did you lie to me about Hailey? About your break-up with her?"

Jade felt as though a rock had fallen on her, she felt the weight of it pressing her deeper into the ground. She saw herself sinking, trying to stay afloat, on the ground. She felt her heart racing, beating so fast she feared Grace would hear her. She drew herself back and sat the way Grace sat, her back bent, her elbow pressed against her thighs, her hands laced together, swallowing the saliva that had gathered in her mouth. She could taste the bile and sorrow in it.

There was silence for a moment, and they sat in the living room, listening to the audible sounds of people's voices coming from outside and cars hooting and honking down the street. A moment of great despair between the two of them.

"Hailey didn't deserve it. She didn't deserve you" Grace said softly.

Jade was thoughtful, "I was scared, Grace."

"And you went on to cheat on her?!" She turned toward Jade.

"I went on to find love! Someone who would love me the way I wanted to!"

"And, Hailey didn't give that to you?"

Jade stared stiffed-face, her eyes unblinking, and her

chest heaving as well. She sighed.

"Hailey loved you, and you had to go ruin it all."

"It was already ruined when she started loving you!"

"It was because of you I left Hailey in the first place!"

"Oh please, if I hadn't shown you I knew about you two, you would still be kissing her under your sheet!
You keep doing it in every relationship you have and I feel I am an accomplice to your betrayals because you call me your fucking 'best friend'."

An icy silence fell over the room, and Grace paused with a stunned look on her face, her eyes fixed on Jade. She was getting angry and Jade's words were making it worse. Grace passed a moist tongue between her dried lips, and had it in a tight form. She was tired.

"I think you need to leave, Jade." Grace said.

Jade felt weaker than before, weaker than she had felt, watching Grace throw those words at her. The words, she hated it, her heart wretched and tightened on hearing it. They were like blades, sharp and cold, piercing through her skin, pushing deeper and deeper till it had reached her organs. She felt completely dejected.

"So, that's how it's going to be?" she asked in a brittled voice.

"Please, leave, Jade." Grace repeated.

Jade's lips had gone dried as well, she moistened them with her tongue, and got up. She stood over Grace, watching her clear, pale face that was equally scathed with pain, and when she saw Grace wasn't going to say anything, she turned to leave.

Grace sat on her couch, her body too numb to do anything. She slumped into the couch, sighing a breath, hot and pained. Grace had her head leaned back, her eyes on the ceiling, she shut them moments after she heard Jade slam the door shut behind her.

"No one deserves to pass through the same hurt twice," were the words Grace said to herself amidst the raging whirlwind of thoughts in her mind.

Chapter Twenty-One

Grace was in another realm, another reality, moving and swaying softly against the air around her. She let herself be driven to a place she found most peace and solace in, a place where her mind was clearer and free from gray clouds that would beat her up.

Grace's mood flowed like a calm river, and so did her hands on her violin as she played herself to relief and freshness within herself. She played with vigor, she played with splendor, and she played with every fiber of her muscles and energy. She played with an exhilarating feeling, diving deep into her soul till she had felt liberated from all that tied her down. It was a moment she enjoyed the most, her violin poised on her shoulder, stroking away on the strings, amongst her band, creating music that would bring out another part of them, a part that was the same as the air they breathe.

Slowly, the colorful sounds and melody that they were creating started to fade, receding back into the instruments they were playing with. Soon, the final key was pushed, Tom's piano keys, and the music came to an end.

"Okay, this is great. All of you were amazing, there's no

doubt in my mind our audience won't love this." Danny's voice rose up over their heads.

"Of course, they will, we are the Jazzlins. We create music that speaks to the soul." Chris boasted, laughing contently.

They all agreed with him. Their band was fast becoming a sensation in their city, and they have been getting numerous calls from event hosts, asking them for a performance at their events. And in 5 day's time, they will be going for another performance, this time, for a better pay. A billionaire had ordered their services, to perform for him at his house, in front of friends. The job was too good to let go.

"That is right, Chris, and soon, we will all be living the lives we have always wanted." said Sara, enthused by the feeling of fame.

Grace sat where she would always sit, on the couch in the corner. She was listening as others chatted about their ambitions and their slow rise to fame, and she watched as they all beamed at the idea of having to perform in front of an audience. She shared the same aspiration with them, the same feeling, but had decided to step aside, watching like a spectator during a football game.

However, she had other things to do. She brought out her phone and texted Hailey. A smile appeared on her face as she tapped the words, a jittery sensation pouring deep into her. She felt more relaxed texting her now that Hailey was single.

– "How's your stay so far?" Grace sent.

She saw Hailey tying, and her heart raced even faster, her face glued to the screen. She didn't even notice when Jeff left the studio, bidding everyone a good bye.

Hailey's reply came in.

– "Boring."

– "Why?! Homesick?"

Grace started worrying.

– "Not really, it's just so lonely here."

Grace could hear Hailey's soft, fluid voice behind those words, and stared at the phone with excitement all over her face.

– "Aww, need some company?"

– "Absolutely!!! Wish you were here, Grace."

Grace paused as she was about to tap a reply, seeing Hailey's reply made her feel a bit flushed and her face went pink with a blush. This was the moment she had been waiting for.

– "I wish so too."

She thought it a bold move to have sent that message, ready for whatever will come afterwards. Though she believed Hailey felt what she felt, she decided it would be best going all in.

– "Tell you what, Hailey, when you come back, I will treat you to somewhere I have always enjoyed going to. I know you will absolutely love it."

– "That would be great, Grace. I can't wait!!!"
Grace let out a small laugh, putting a hand over her mouth to hold it back. She heard a voice call out to her, and she raised her head to it. It was Danny, and he was about to lock the studio.

"Uhh, Grace, sorry to spoil your–"

"It's alright, Danny, I will be going now."

She tapped on her phone to send one last message.

– "I'll be going now, talk to you later."

As she left the studio, she and Danny exchanged smiles, though Danny's was the brightest. Grace went home with a glow that would illuminate any room she entered, her mood was unrestrained, she had an aura that exuded a benign confidence in her.

As she walked home, cold shivers kept running down her spine and all over her body, her hair kept standing on end, imagining a moment with Hailey again, by her side, just the way it had been. A bold step she was willing to take toward making whole what she had once damaged.

***

Jade walked briskly, trotting up a pathway that led to an elevator. She wore a white, button-up shirt and a black trouser that hung right above her ankles, under the trouser was a pair of black, flat heels and she was on her way to her boss' office. She walked with a sullen expression that would loosen up in a fake smile whenever she saw her colleagues. Her mind hasn't been at peace, and she felt it was time she needed a rest, to clear her head more.

After a few minutes and lots of steps and fake smiles, she reached the office. She stood at the door, and gave it a knock. A voice told her to come in, and she did. She walked into a big space with dark brown floors and an interior that had brown and grey as their colors. It was the CEO's office, and Jade had always admired how smooth and quaint the office looked like.

The owner of the office sat behind a desk near a glass window, a plump man with a fat face and a protruding belly and inquisitive, pale brown eyes. He wore a black blazer on a white shirt and watched as Jade approached him.

"Miss Jade, is anything the matter?" his voice rang throughout the room.

Jade walked to her boss, her hands clasped together in anxiety below her waist line. She moved with a mild trembling to her gait, and wore a troubled, gloomy look on her face. The office was bright with a splurge of light, but none of it could do anything to make her mood any brighter.

"Yes, sir, I actually came to ask you for something." she said softly, almost pleading with her tone.

"And, what would that be?" he asked with an arched brow, sitting back on his chair to get a better look at her.

"I would," she paused, taking in a deep breath, "I would like to ask for a leave from work. I feel like I have been underperforming lately, and would like to have a break from work."

Her boss looked at her thoughtfully, his hand laced together on his belly, whirling in his black chair. He groaned and pushed his fleshy body forward, placing his arms on the table.

"Okay, Jade. You can go, but you have only a week to get back in shape, you hear me?"

"I do, sir."

Jade went back to her office desk, got her things ready to go. Her mind was still a muddled mess, and she tried to keep herself from falling a few times. She would feel dizzy and her balance would be lost, she felt terrible and she couldn't place what exactly was wrong.

A moment later, a colleague came in to join her. She was a woman with a light complexion, small figure and face, and looked about the same age as Jade, in her mid-thirties. She stood before Jade with an affectionate look on her face, standing near the door, and was waiting for Jade to notice her presence. Jade eventually did.

"Hey," She said.

"Amy, what are you doing here?" Jade asked with a perplexed look.

"I am here to see you," she replied, "I have been seeing you lately, and have noticed how…messed up you look. Even now, you still look messed up. What's wrong, Jade?" she asked.

Jade went back to what she was doing, "It's nothing, Amy. I just need some rest, that's all."

"Hmm, whatever it may be, Jade, don't let it eat you up too deep. Know that things can always be repaired when broken, even if it seems irreparable. It can still be repaired." she said to her, "I have a feeling you are having an issue with your girlfriend, what's her name again? Hailey? I think Hailey. That is why I am telling you this." she further added.

Jade made to leave, walking up to Amy, "Thank you, Amy. I will be going now," she said, staring into Amy's face with a disinterested face.

Jade walked out on Amy, and out of the office, and wished Amy hadn't come to meet her. She cussed under her breath for it, and got a little annoyed. Amy, however, felt no hurt toward Jade's actions. She was expecting it as Jade didn't look like she was in the mood. Amy only smiled, and let Jade walk out, without saying a word.

As Jade walked to her, she thought of what Amy said. Though she was still angry, she felt Amy had a point. Jade sat in her car, thinking about her stand with Hailey, she realized Hailey wasn't the one she missed, she loved her, but Hailey was already gone even before they broke up.

She let out a stiff sigh, and picked up her phone. She scrolled through it and had gotten a number, and she dialed it, placing a call. Sadly, it didn't go through, and she had to drop a voice message.

"Hey, Grace… I just want to say I'm sorry. I am sorry for everything I have done, and not acknowledge how much of a friend you've been to me all these years. I realize I have been a bad friend, and I would like to change that from now on. I just want us to be as we were, to come back again. My life has not been so good, and I need you again."

She dropped the phone, and froze to a spot, staring wide-eyed into the parking lot through her car windshield. She felt a sudden rush of relief for something she had always wanted to do but couldn't. She had her fears and her doubts, and with a bold move, that has been dispersed into the air. She felt unburdened from it, and for the first time in a while, she felt good.

Moments later, she heard her phone ring, and she turned to it quicker than she had realized. Jade picked it up, and peered at it. It was Grace calling. She gasped.